HEAR MY VOICE

By David Vaughan

JANTAR PUBLISHING

London 2019

First published in Great Britain in 2018 by
Jantar Publishing Ltd
www.jantarpublishing.com

David Vaughan
HEAR MY VOICE

A CIP catalogue record for this book is available from the British Library
ISBN 978-0-9934467-3-3

CONTENTS

FOREWORD

It is 1938 and Hitler is spreading his poison through Central Europe. With the world's press corps descending on Prague, a young man from London arrives in the city as an interpreter. He witnesses dramatic and unsettling events, as Germany sucks Austria and then Czechoslovakia into its orbit, and little by little he loses his grip on reality. His job is to translate, yet he finds himself lost for words. Truth will prevail, but whose truth will it be?

At the heart of this novel is the new medium of radio. Omnipresent yet intangible, it provides a background of unstable, shifting and competing narratives, shattering time and distance. In 1938 radio was as radically new as the social media today, shaping events at every level and every moment, informing and misinforming, making and breaking political careers, creating its own parallel realities.

When I first started researching and writing on this subject over a decade ago, it seemed that I was opening a window onto a distant, faded past that was very different from our own time. Even the word "propaganda" seemed oddly anachronistic in a world where the internet offered so many sources and perspectives. But the warning signs were already there. History does not repeat itself, but patterns of behaviour do. In 1937 the great American broadcaster Edward R Murrow was talking about radio when he said that it "reflects the hatreds, the jealousies and ambitions of those men and governments that control it." He added that it "can become a powerful force for mutual understanding between nations, but not until we have made it so." The same can be applied to the electronic media of today.

In 2008, coinciding with the seventieth anniversary of the Munich Agreement, I wrote *Battle for the Airwaves*, in which I looked at how the Nazis used radio to stir up passions, to spread rumours and fears, to put pressure on politicians and diplomats, and to bully and flatter people into compliance. The pressure was unrelenting and consistent, and as their poisoned words seeped into the language of those they were addressing, the unthinkable became acceptable. Truth became the "will of the people" in service of the leader. Diplomacy became a hybrid war, creating realities on the ground by force or threat, and Europe's democrats, with their language of compromise and reasoned argument, looked weak in the face of forces that seemed to have history on their side. Talk of common interests, collective security and even the premise that "truth will prevail" – the national motto of Czechoslovakia – seemed inadequate and outdated. Journalists lost confidence and found themselves at a loss for words. A few continued to fight for the values they held sacred and some were to pay with their lives.

A decade has passed since I wrote *Battle for the Airwaves*. As if time were going backwards, 1938 seems much closer today. The word "propaganda" has re-entered our everyday vocabulary. In many places the techniques of persuasion and manipulation used by Hitler and Goebbels are being applied to the electronic media of our own time. "Radio knows no borders" were the words on one advertising poster from the 1930s. The same can be applied a hundredfold to today's electronic media.

Any discussion of propaganda only makes sense if we talk about what it does to those to whom it is addressed and how it breaks down their ability to read their world. That is what we see in *Hear My Voice*. This is not a historical novel in the usual sense. The story is not driven by the actors playing out their lives before a backdrop that provides local and historical colour. Instead they are defined and shaped by the setting. They are carried with the ebb and flow of events, they are manipulated, confused, disillusioned, seduced. Some are themselves manipulators and seducers, many lose their way, and a few show a remarkable resilience. The book is built around real events and places, and most of the people who appear in the story really lived. They are journalists, politicians and diplomats, but also ordinary people who find themselves drawn into history at a moment of deep crisis. Although this is a work of the imagination, I have tried to portray them as honestly and faithfully as possible. I would like to think that I would have been one of the few who refused to bend with the times, but history tells me that I am probably wrong.

This is not a long book, but it does have a large cast, and that is why it includes an appendix with a few words about some of the historical figures who appear in the story.

David Vaughan
Prague, March 2019

ACKNOWLEDGEMENTS

Many people helped me with this book and I cannot name them all here, but I would like to thank some: Alena Zemančíková from Czech Radio, who helped me at every stage of writing the Czech version of this book *Slyšte můj hlas* (Radioservis 2014); Joe Cook and Pavla Horáková for their role in the pre-history of the book; Jane Kirwan, Marcus Gärtner, Alex Went, Katrin Bock, Hannah Vaughan, Sarah Vaughan, Clara Farmer, Sarah Perry and Simon Mawer, for looking at the manuscript at various stages and giving me honest and useful advice; my publisher Michael Tate for his infectious energy and enthusiasm. I would also like to thank the Villa Decius in Krakow for providing me with a quiet place to work at a crucial stage in the writing of this book. I owe a great debt to Sydney "Bill" Morrell, whose book *I Saw the Crucifixion* (P. Davies 1939) was published just after he witnessed the events of 1938. It is a wonderful work of engaged reporting from the eye of the storm. Several passages in this book draw very closely from his account. I have often imagined Bill with his fox terrier Pop at his side, stubbornly refusing to rely on second-hand accounts as he travelled through Czechoslovakia in search of the truth.

Every one that is of the truth heareth my voice.

JOHN 18:37

Radio is the most influential and important intermediary between the spiritual movement and the nation, between the idea and the people.

JOSEPH GOEBBELS, 1938

NUREMBERG before the war is set in my memory. As I draw closer I see the details carved into the wood and stone of the old houses, and I see myself as a young man, walking open-eyed through the streets on a clear afternoon. It must have been December 1937. I was enjoying a few hours' rest on my way to Prague. It felt as though the glow of the early winter sun would warm the old houses forever.

*

In the city I entered twelve-and-a-half years later, even the fragments I recognised were quite foreign. In places where I recalled buildings, trees had grown and birds were singing. Buildings stood where there used to be birds and trees. I remember that I felt anxious, almost unwell.

I walked through the suburbs heading south. More of the old city survived here. Somewhere among the villas, with their gardens turned over to vegetables, a child was practising scales on the piano, and for a while the sun came out.

It was almost evening when I reached the Zeppelinfeld. This was a place that I knew, not because I had been there before – during my few hours here in 1937 the Party rallies had been the last thing on my mind – but because, a few months after that first visit, I had been carried there on the airwaves, on a September evening when the Führer's voice played on the world's eardrums.

*

Another forty years have passed. I am an old man and I would like that sound to fade into a forgotten past. Instead it is drawing closer, humming loudly in my head.

Phonomotors and Electric Birds

I arrived in Prague not long before Christmas 1937, nearly a year before the drama that came to be known as the Munich Crisis. The shops were being decorated and on the corners of many of the streets there were big tanks filled with carp ready to be taken home to kill and eat on Christmas Eve. They made me think of an old picture book that my mother used to show me when I was small. The city was pretty, like the city in the book, and in many ways similar to the Nuremberg I had just left. Given the uncertain times, I was surprised by the good cheer in the air.

On my first evening I went to the pub U Kocoura to meet Ivan Jelínek from Radiojournal. I found him straight away, sitting in a corner, scribbling with a pencil into a small notebook, a half-litre of beer on the table in front of him, his hair rebellious. He waved to me to join him and immediately another beer appeared.

At first I sipped nervously, wiping the froth from my upper lip with my sleeve. I was little used to drinking, but Jelínek knew how to make me feel at home and soon our conversation was flowing as freely as the beer. As we chatted it was hard to imagine him as a news journalist, one of Czechoslovak radio's rising stars; our conversation kept drifting back to poetry, which he wove into the conversation with little or no warning. I had always felt a little self-conscious about my love for books and was happy in the company of someone to whom verse came as naturally as the air he breathed. In the coming months I was to meet several people who shared his delight at the play of language and languages, but none of them quite to the same degree as Jelínek. The conversation jumped from Sanskrit to the ballet of dialects in his native South Moravia. He broke into song "*V tem Kyjově v krajním domě, tam sa šije mundúr pro mě*... this one's from Kyjov, my home town," he explained, "it's about a lad parting from his girl as he goes off to war ... they're sewing my uniform ... *Pód' má milá výprovod', eště je malá chvilka do dňa*... but we still have a little time till sunrise."

He raised his arms above his head and I thought he was going to stand up and break into dance. He seemed to be carried by the music of words, yet, as I listened to him talk about the changes unfolding around us, I realised that Ivan Jelínek was no dreamer. He was acutely aware of the power of words to corrupt.

"In the time of Emperor Rudolph, the alchemists thought they could turn base metal into gold. They failed. But today we are seeing words forged into steel." He leaned towards me. "Look at how technology is changing our lives." He went on in a whisper, as if betraying a state secret. "And a great deal of it is down to one word. Radio. *Wireless, rozhlas, Rundfunk.* Call it what you will. Words are flying through the air with the power of a thousand bombers." By now he was whispering loudly like an actor who wants to make sure he can be heard in the gods. He switched suddenly to an unmistakable staccato, and he raised both hands, fingers outstretched, as if holding a giant crystal ball before him, imitating with uncanny precision the tone and gestures of Reichsminister Goebbels: "Some of us, you see, are a step ahead …" His voice was rising to a climax, "We will bring to the microphone the mightiest spiritual elements of the nation … making radio into the most multifaceted means of expressing the wishes … the needs … the longings … and the hopes of our great revolution. *Sieg Heil!*" At that point Jelínek burst out laughing, and at the next table a couple of heads turned. Goebbels, mixed with the beer, was beginning to make my head spin, I felt myself sinking into a queasy, uneasy melancholy. Jelínek must have noticed because, suddenly and unexpectedly, he changed his tone again and took off on the wings of poetry, "The whole world plays on your eardrums … you become a source of electricity … phonomotors and electric birds … fly up to the stars and then return." He laughed. "Do you know Nezval's *Edison*? It's really rather good. Yes, there are people on our side who know all about radio too."

We finished our beer, said our farewells and I headed unsteadily over the cobbles in the direction of an old house with a hipped roof, half hidden between Újezd and the park at Petřín, where I was renting two dark, low-ceilinged rooms.

Jelínek called after me, "Come into the radio on Christmas Eve … before six o'clock. You'll see electric birds fly up to the stars …"

A Land-Locked Sea Captain

Whitechapel, where I spent my childhood, was just east of the City of London. It was a Babel of different languages; we were close to the docks, the first stopping place for people who had come to London from the furthest corners of Europe and beyond. Everyone dreamed of moving to the leafier parts a few stations out from Liverpool Street and if my father had lived a little longer, no doubt we would have moved there too. Chadwell Heath, Seven Kings or Harold Wood ... as a child I rehearsed these names in my head and dreamed of oak forests and medieval knights.

In the end I was not too bothered that we had stayed within sight of the cranes of the docks. The area was always busy; it was mostly Jewish, and as Catholics we were a little exotic, although the Irish helped to keep up numbers. We would speak a mixture of German and English with our Jewish neighbours and they spoke Yiddish with each other, which I understood without much difficulty. My parents had come from Prague, although my father was originally from Lower Silesia. His mother tongue was German, my mother spoke Czech and they were unusual in making sure that my little sister Anna and I grew up speaking both languages. Apart from that – and our rather dubious popery – we were pretty much English, leading quiet lives in genteel poverty.

Being something of a polyglot proved useful. As soon as I left school I found work as an interpreter and translator. I must have been the best-paid fifteen-year-old in our street and most of the credit was due to my mother. She worked in the local library and had a librarian's sense of doing things in a proper, thorough and orderly fashion. Anna and I joked that she might introduce a card index at home to keep our lives in order. But I shall always be thankful to her for her stubborn insistence that we kept our languages.

*

My first encounter with Edgar Young was some four years later, at Toynbee Hall, where lectures were held regularly for the betterment of the East End's working classes, as the Victorians would have put it. The hall was an incongruous neo-Jacobean building, like a country house that had landed by mistake amid the narrow soot-blackened brick terraces of Whitechapel. It was a chilly, wet evening in October 1937. Inside, a large fire was crackling in the fireplace and above it hung a large portrait of an Anglican priest and his wife in a heavy gilt frame. I looked into the flames and for a moment imagined myself as Sherlock Holmes, solving a country-house mystery. An oddly assorted crew had come to hear the former sea-captain and Great War hero talk about Czechoslovakia.

Captain Young was a socialist, known for his outspoken views, but his war record had earned him the respect of politicians from both left and right. He was tall and gaunt with the stiffly upright bearing and polished vowels of his class, quite at odds with his politics. His manner was boyish, and perhaps that was why I plucked up courage to talk to him after the lecture.

I never managed to work out what inspired a man who had spent much of his life at sea to take an interest in such an uncompromisingly landlocked country as Czechoslovakia. Young had fallen romantically in love with all things Czech and I suspect that it came from his gentleman's sense that it was always right to support the underdog. His lecture was about the role of socialism in Czechoslovakia and the need for the democratic states of Europe to stand together. Britain and her Empire had a moral obligation to help Czechoslovakia in her hour of need; we must show solidarity with a land where millions of workers are ready to drop tools and take up arms against dictators. The applause was long and loud. He ended by talking about his planned visit to Prague and the Sudetenland.

I think he was half joking when he asked if anyone in the audience might be able to come and interpret for him. My third-hand suit could have housed two of me and I stuttered terribly as I told him of my language skills. But with a broad smile, he settled it there and then, shaking my hand for ages as if to prove he meant it. We arranged another meeting. Over the next few days I was contacted by several other newspapermen, all of whom wanted to see Czechoslovakia for themselves. More or less by chance, an awkward and rather bookish nineteen-year-old had ended up as a not-quite-official interpreter for the British press in Prague.

*

While Anna and I were washing up in our tiny kitchen, Máma put her head round the door. Abruptly, as if she had been rehearsing her words, she asked in English if I really thought it was wise to go abroad. These were uncertain times. I pretended not to have heard, feeling a little offended, and busied myself with drying the plates. This was an opportunity to see more of the world. I was no longer a child. Anna said nothing.

By the time we had finished in the kitchen, I felt a little ashamed. Anna went straight into the front room to listen to the wireless, but I was surprised to see our mother sitting at the little dining table, distracted, turning a wooden napkin ring in her hand as if checking for some irregularity. I sat down opposite her and was surprised when she put her hand gently on my arm and tears came to her eyes. She began to talk about Prague, moving between Czech and English, naming the sites I should see and recalling places from her own childhood: Petřín, when the cherry trees were in blossom; the pond at Břevnov where she would skate with her school friends; the wealthy old German-speaking ladies wrapped in fur, promenading with their little dogs in front of Franz Joseph Station. Again, I felt a little ashamed. "Take good care of yourself. It will not always be easy," she said, and then stood up, the librarian once again, carefully cataloguing the cups and plates that Anna had just put back in the dresser and slipping the napkin ring neatly into its rightful place.

The Garrulous Waves

It was bitterly cold, with powder snow blowing in swirls on the pavement outside the Radiojournal building in Fochova Street. By a bit of electronic magic, the words *Veselé Vánoce* – Merry Christmas – were flashing onto the pavement from the window of the photographic shop by the main entrance. A small crowd was defying the cold, as if by standing outside they could capture some of the magic of the airwaves and be part of a rare event; Ivan Jelínek greeted me like an old friend and whisked me through the double doors. We hopped into the paternoster lift. It was already nearly six. In the control room the party atmosphere was more palpable still, and the Christmas tree in the corner seemed the least festive element in the whole place. Engineers were running around, it was a bit like being in a telephone exchange; they connected and disconnected cables. Red and green lights flashed, telephone receivers were picked up and put down, headphones were plugged in and pulled out. Static could be heard from loudspeakers and the voice of the presenter in the studio further down the corridor … *Can you hear me America?*

The young Jelínek, looking a little ill-kempt with his hair flying up to the stars like the electric birds in the poem, was standing rather incongruously next to the radio director Ladislav Šourek who, in his expensive English suit, looked like a dapper New York businessman. Jelínek told me what was going on. We were trying to establish a radio bridge to America. The thousands of miles that separated us would disappear and with them all the darkness that lay in between. The great Bengali poet, Rabindranath Tagore, had just sent a message from Santiniketan. Now Albert Einstein was to address us from Princeton. One of the sound engineers held up a finger for us to be quiet and we listened, as a professor from Prague's Technical University read a message to Einstein from the ninety-year-old Czech inventor of the arc-lamp, František Křižík. I could just see through the soundproof glass into the studio. He talked of how science and technology had cut down distances across the world and how he had faith in progress and a happy future for mankind. And then, as if Mephistopheles had been waiting for his cue, the shortwave bridge broke down. Engineers rushed around, trying to maintain a signal. The presenter, Zdenka Walló, continued from the studio …

Can you hear me, Professor Einstein?…

An electronic hum. She continued in Czech…

Voláme márně Albertu Einsteinovi …

All we could hear from America was a roar of static. I shut my eyes and found myself in the middle of an Atlantic storm. From time to time I picked out a fragment of voice or music, the band playing on, as the ship went down.

Jelínek turned to me, grinning grimly and I was not surprised when he broke into verse, "Before him the endless ocean roared. The garrulous waves ceaselessly talked of hidden treasures, mocking the ignorance that knew not their meaning." He laughed out loud. "The poet hit the nail on the head. The garrulous waves are certainly doing their best to keep us in ignorance tonight! Those lines are from Tagore, aptly enough – *The Wandering Madman*."

In the end we did not get to hear Einstein. He resorted to sending his message by telegram and it was read out from the studio:

It is hard to dare to place one's hopes in mankind's will to justice. But the hope remains that a coming generation, out of healthy egoism, will manage through sober consideration, to force an enduring pacification of the world through powerful and honest cooperation between nations. I look forward to and envy this generation. Heartfelt thanks to my kindred spirits in Prague, and I enclose my deepfelt desire, that the example you are giving will work to the wellbeing of all.

Despite all the technical hitches, the presenter came out of the studio beaming, congratulated on all sides. The radio director Šourek smiled and shook her hand, "Good work, Zdenka."

A few seconds later, Šourek turned to Jelínek and spoke in quite a different tone, as if suddenly cut by a glass wall from the excitement around him. His words were sober, and his voice sounded tired. "I was at the international radio exhibition in Berlin when Einstein opened it in 1930. We were surrounded by all the latest technical innovations – radio was going to change the world."

He waved in the direction of the equipment in the studio around us. "At the time I was inspired by Einstein's words: that democracy and technology were one ... today's engineers were the fathers of the communication that makes democracy possible ... unlimited communication ... vast networks of people of goodwill ... overcoming centuries of ignorance and prejudice ..." Šourek repeated the gesture, as if looking for material confirmation of his words. "And do you know who opened the same exhibition three years later?"

"Der kleine Herr Reichspropagandaminister," Jelínek replied promptly, imitating Goebbels with the same uncanny precision as in the pub. He concluded with a grotesque little dance of death.

"Indeed." Šourek went on, "Mr Goebbels really does love radio. He has made the Reich's radio network function perfectly; he's swept through the bureaucracy, the petty political bickering that we face every day here in Radiojournal and created a broadcasting machine that is aligned to their national revolution. And do you know what?" He paused, as if wondering whether to go on. "It's not just propaganda and political ranting – it really is good radio. People want to listen. It makes them feel good. And do you know what is most unnerving of all? It gives them a future."

"And what do we have on our part?" Jelínek chipped in. "Messages of goodwill ... and even they are lost in the ether." He put his hand in front of his eyes, pretending to grope around like blind justice. I was taken aback by the bitter irony with which he added, "Truth will prevail." Šourek gave him a stern look, shrugged his shoulders and left.

The Sea-Coast of Bohemia

It wasn't long before I was able to see the impact of Herr Goebbels' experiment for myself. Edgar Young sent me a telegram that he was on his way to Prague. At Wilson Station I spotted him as soon as he stepped off the train. His inimitable naval bearing made him float above the landlocked families with suitcases, tumbling out of the carriages. He sailed through the crowd and greeted me with the enthusiasm of a prep school boy coming home for half term, tipping the porter generously. We were to set off for Liberec the following afternoon. Young wanted to waste no time before seeing the German-speaking areas of North and West Bohemia. But before we left I did manage to introduce him to František Kraus from the radio's shortwave broadcasts who agreed that Young should give a talk for Radiojournal's British and North American service when we returned.

We borrowed a car in Prague and spent a week travelling between Liberec and Karlovy Vary, stopping in every other village. I enjoyed the driving. I had only taken lessons a few weeks before, in preparation for the trip, and was still slightly uncertain on the icy roads in the hills. At least they drove on the left, unlike in Germany. Young joked that we would be able to recognise the Hitler supporters, as they'd be the ones driving on the other side. I laughed nervously.

Nearly everyone – Czech or German – was glad to talk to us. They seemed pleased that someone from outside was interested in how they lived, and the tall British naval officer added an element of dignity to it all. Again and again we were invited for *koláčky* or *Kaffee und Kuchen* in the warm parlour of one of the log-built cottages that dotted the winter landscape.

The rolling countryside had a fairytale prettiness to it, but our impression was not a happy one. This was a landscape of industrial villages, but most of the factories were idle. In several towns we visited the labour exchange and every time the picture was the same: high unemployment and little hope that things might get better. Unemployment relief was as good as non-existent, even lower, Young noted, than in Britain.

Sympathisers with the revolution in Germany, most of them boys and young men of about my age or even younger, made their presence felt on every corner and readily told us stories of Czech atrocities, filled with precise detail, exact numbers of victims and where and when each incident had occurred. They would follow a pattern. On such-and-such a day at such-and-such a time, Czech gendarmes from the police station in such-and-such a village had opened fire on a group of unarmed German civilians. One was killed, sometimes two, several more were injured and brought to the hospital in such-and-such a town at such-and-such a time. It very soon became clear that the source of these details was German radio, broadcasting from across the border in the Reich. When we tried to follow up the stories we never had any luck and I realised very quickly that for the people who were recounting them to us it was not important whether they were actually *true*. If you wanted to believe, you believed them, and even if you did not believe them, the effect was the same. After all, they *could have* happened.

On several occasions, when we were sitting in a village pub warming ourselves by the big tile stove somewhere away from the bigger towns, we caught glimpses of a different world. The talk was still of the injustices of the government in Prague – "Even we Germans have a right to a place in the sun," was the expression we heard again and again – but only rarely was the tone one of threat. "We brought European culture to the Slavs," one village official from Konrad Henlein's Nazi-sympathising Sudeten German Party told us, and I braced myself for a lecture on the historic calling of the German nation. But that was not what he was saying at all. "You know, we are a bit different here. We always have been. Something like a bridge between the German and Slav worlds."

"You won't find that in *Mein Kampf*," Young muttered into his beer so that only I could hear.

"We're nothing but *böhmische Dörfer* to them," the party official went on, gesticulating in what I took to be the rough direction of Prague and then Berlin. And we certainly felt a world away from both capitals. *"Böhmische Dörfer,"* I explained to Young, "means Bohemian villages. It's the German expression for something you really don't understand." Young raised his glass. "All Greek to me!"

"Exactly."

Relations between local Czechs and Germans seemed far from friendly, but at no time did we have the impression that civil war was about to break out. A slightly reserved and prickly courtesy was more the rule, among Czechs and Germans alike. "Almost English," as Young put it. If this gave us some reassurance, the self-confidence of people around the Sudeten German Party leader Henlein most certainly did not. They acted as if everything already belonged to them.

I was hoping to get a chance to see Henlein himself. I knew he was a former sports teacher and that he had managed to win huge support since Hitler had come to power across the border, but I had no idea by what magic he had done so.

As I drove us back to Prague, Young tried to formulate his thoughts. He was holding a copy of *Die Zeit*, the Henlein party paper. "Have you noticed that all the local papers, at least the ones that people actually read, are in the hands of Henlein supporters? My German's not great, but I can see that they're full of the same sort of thing that we're hearing from the Reich radio stations."

"I think you're right." We discussed the latest Sudeten German Party boycott of Czechoslovak goods and Jewish-owned firms. Young recalled our trip to meet the director of a textile manufactory in Liberec. A jovial and extrovert fifty-year-old in Sudeten German Party uniform – it was strange in itself to see a factory owner in uniform – he had greeted us enthusiastically. As he took us down to the factory floor, he enthused about the new Germany. "We want nothing more than the right to our own *German* world view," he said in a reasonable tone. "You only have to see how the German Chancellor has rebuilt the towns on the other side of the border. And the Czechs won't even let us Germans work on the railways unless we can tell them the names of the dogs in their damned fairy-tales. I'm not joking. They have these special language tests. And do you think it's the Czechs who are buying what we produce here? They don't care."

"But is it true that you have sacked all employees who are unable to show a Sudeten German Party card?" Young asked with his boyish innocence, sheltering behind my cautious translation. The man shrugged, "In the end it's not about parties, it's about *knowing who you are*. We are not willing to reduce ourselves to the role of villains in someone else's fairy-tale."

I drove us cautiously through the snow-covered landscape. Occasionally we spotted children sledging and roe deer in the open fields.

We stopped at one last German village, one of the few, we had been told, where the mayor was not a member of the Sudeten German Party. We found him in his little office just off the village square, easily identifiable with the Czechoslovak tricolour still flying above the porch. He was just how the Englishman imagines a German bureaucrat. "I wonder if his wife irons him every morning," Young whispered, although he himself was just as immaculately turned out. The mayor greeted us very politely and introduced his secretary, a young Czech woman, who spent the whole of our visit busily typing letters. He sat us down on the other side of his polished desk and began to paint a picture that was as apocalyptic as his desk was ordered. He admitted that he had no great affection for Czechoslovakia, but *order must prevail*. Henlein and his people are creating disorder, they are bullying people, marching around in self-styled military uniforms and ... *they are disloyal*. This last transgression was the most unforgivable of all and would lead to chaos and destruction. I tried to guess the mayor's age.

As a young man he had probably fought in the 14–18 war for the old Viennese order with much the same loyalty as the socialist Young had fought for the British Empire.

The mayor took us outside. The sun was shining on the fresh snow. He wanted to show us the view from the hill behind the village. A landscape of mixed forests, stretching far in all directions. As if dictating an inventory of his homeland, he repeated the name of each hill, each village, first in German, Holzbach, Endersgrün, Wirbelstein … then in Czech, Plavno, Ondřejov, Meluzína … Each name was as rooted in the landscape as the trees themselves.

We said our goodbyes with a polite handshake. Young and I had an overwhelming sense of sadness as we watched the mayor walk alone down the snow-covered path back to the village. I felt afraid for people like him. I doubted he had made plans to escape when the worst came. It would not have occurred to him.

The next day Young gave his talk for Radiojournal's short-wave broadcasts. At the end he appealed to listeners to visit Czechoslovakia.

> *It is unfortunate that Czechoslovakia is known to most foreigners largely, if not entirely, through the propaganda of her enemies. The Czechoslovaks are only now beginning to realise the dangerous effects of the new technique of propaganda, which consists in telling lies and half-truths with such conviction and consistency that even the victims begin to wonder what is really the truth. They have yet to devise an effective counter to it, and in the meanwhile it would be a good thing if more foreigners were to visit the republic, to see for themselves how things really are, and to tell their countrymen the plain truth.*

The Walls of the Temple

It was a crisp winter's day when Young and I visited the British Embassy in Thunovská Street. The thick snow had us both singing *Good King Wenceslas* as we tramped across the square below the old Jesuit seminary, although by now it was well after Christmas. Young was amused when I proceeded to sing it in Czech…

Na Štěpána dobrý král
Václav z okna hledí,
všude kam se podívá,
závěje a ledy.
Svítil měsíc a byl mráz,
pálil jako divý,
a vtom spatří chudáka,
jak tam sbírá dříví.

The welcome we were given at the Embassy was as icy as the weather, even though they had no choice but to receive Young politely. His pedigree and war record guaranteed that. I had been told by several of the people I had met at Radiojournal that the legacy of Joseph Addison's time as ambassador here was still very strong and that the mission had a reputation for being decidedly chilly towards its hosts. "The kind of people who dine in the kitchen," had been Addison's take on the Czech nation. His reports to Whitehall had been in a similar spirit, or so I was told by Young, who had friends in the Foreign Office.

We were more than a little surprised to find the British Ambassador to Germany, Nevile Henderson, at the Embassy, apparently in Prague on some business of Chamberlain's. Later that evening, Young and I worked out what had brought him to the city. Given that Anthony Eden had just resigned as Foreign Secretary in protest against Chamberlain's decision to side with Italy over Mussolini's invasion of Abyssinia, he was in all probability here to make sure that the Prague mission was firmly behind the Prime Minister. It was said that Henderson's views of the Czechs were close to those of Addison, and he certainly made no secret of his admiration for the Führer. I was too timid to join in myself, but I listened closely to Henderson's conversation with Young. How did the Sudeten crisis – or the *Czech question*, as the British papers liked to call it – look from the perspective of Berlin? Henderson was in provocative and undiplomatic mood. When Young started talking about our recent trip to the Sudetenland and warned of the depth of infiltration from Nazi Germany, Henderson interrupted curtly,

"However badly Germany behaves, it does not make the rights of the Sudeten any less justifiable." He had fired his first shot across the sea captain's bow. "You know only too well that it's a clear question of their right to self-government." Another salvo. "Never again are those blocks of Germans on Germany's frontier going to be misgoverned by Czechs as they have been during the past twenty years. That seems to me inconceivable and we have no earthly or heavenly right to force them to be so." He paused. "The Teuton and the Slav are irreconcilable …"

"I'm sorry?" For a minute Young was lost for words.

"… just as are the Briton and the Slav. When Mackenzie King was over for the Imperial Conference last year, we had a long talk about these things. He told me that the Slavs in Canada never assimilated and never became good citizens."

Young returned fire. "Are Henlein's people being good citizens?"

"Are you trying to tell me that they are not being provoked?" Henderson exploded. "Whatever the Germans do, one must also condemn President Beneš and his military enthusiasts. Their position is quite untenable … "

Young tried to interrupt again, but Henderson forestalled his complaints …

"Of course one must have sympathy for them, but I cease to have any patience when they try …"

Henderson was looking for the right words with which to cause maximum damage.

"Yes?"

He took a large sip of his whisky.

"… try to behave like … like Samson … and bring down the walls of the Temple to soften the bitterness of their own humiliation. Old President Masaryk would have been great enough to appreciate the hard facts and make the best of them, but Beneš is a small man. That is a fact."

By now Henderson was slightly red in the face. He went on to describe the Czechs as a pig-headed race and before long he was warning of the influence of Jews and Communists on British foreign policy. He looked Edgar Young sternly in the eye as if he were the living embodiment of both these threats and headed off at full steam.

Disease

A terrible unknown malady, a kind of white leprosy, has attacked humanity. The only medical man in the world to find a remedy for the disease, Dr Galén, refuses to part with the secret of his discovery unless the nations of the world agree to perpetual peace. A dictator, a general, has built up an enormous army and it cannot be left idle. War is about to be declared. As the general falls victim to the plague, he accepts the doctor's conditions for a cure. The war is to be terminated. As the doctor is on his way to the palace, armed with the ampules of serum intended for the general, he is lynched by the crowd for refusing to shout, 'Long live the war!' The ampules are scattered and broken, and the crowd, pleased with its work, cries, 'Long live the general!' The general dies, but war is not prevented.

It was as cold as ever and I walked at a brisk pace from my rooms in Újezd across the Legions' Bridge. In the misty half-darkness the National Theatre looked like an Italian Renaissance town hall, marooned on the banks of this northern river. Karel Čapek's new play, *White Disease* was hopelessly sold out and even from a distance I could see the crowds gathering around the entrance. I was lucky to have a ticket thanks to Oswald Bamborough, who had written a review of the play for Radiojournal and had contacts at the theatre. He was an Englishman, an energetic and jovial man in his early thirties, and during his time at the radio he seemed to have made the acquaintance of anyone who was anyone in Prague. "Don't let appearances deceive you," he cautioned when he saw me admiring the building. "It may look old-fashioned but there are exciting things going on here." He enthused about the theatre's artistic director Otokar Fischer and his work with Karel Čapek. "The play will easily match the international success of Čapek's robot play, *RUR*. If I'm not mistaken *RUR* is still running in London." I had not seen the play, but I could hardly have missed all the publicity in the British papers. "There have already been requests to perform *White Disease* in dozens of countries, including Britain, France, Yugoslavia and even Austria. You'll see. It's a perfect reflection of our times. And I expect you've heard that they're making a film too – with the same cast as here at the National Theatre."

"Didn't I read somewhere that the German Embassy sent a protest note, demanding that the filming be stopped?"

"Yes. I'm hoping we'll find out a bit more about that after tonight's show. Will you be able to join us for a drink?"

When we emerged from the theatre over three hours later I was not surprised in the slightest that the play had upset Germany's new generation of rulers. With its story of a warmongering dictator, bullying his neighbours with threats of war, it was so obviously about them. Oswald had seen the production twice before and this time he had busied himself taking notes on details of the stage design. "Did you notice the lighting? It's brilliant, the contrasts of light and darkness ... the luminous scenery ... the white coats of the doctors and the lepers, the birds of death in flight over the city, their immense black wings covering the whole stage. Fantastic." He was so enthusiastic that I could see these great birds sweeping down through the mist over the Vltava.

It was getting colder by the minute and Oswald again urged me to join him for a glass of wine with Otokar Fischer, who as artistic director had first commissioned the play from Čapek. When we turned up at the wine cellar in one of the narrow streets of the New Town, Fischer was already engaged in lively conversation with Ivan Jelínek; they shared a love for poetry and the craft of translation, and had been firm friends ever since Fischer had come to Radiojournal a couple of years earlier to give a talk about translating poetry. At the time the radio's in-house censor had for some reason – that no one now could remember – tried to cut a couple of sentences from his script. Fischer had made short shrift indeed of the censor, who withdrew with his tail between his legs, much to Jelínek's delight.

I had already heard a lot about Fischer. He was probably Czechoslovakia's most erudite scholar of German literature. Ironically, given the contempt in which Germany's new leaders held him, he was a passionate advocate of Czech-German understanding, moving effortlessly and with great eloquence between both languages in his essays and poetry. The new Germans cared nothing for this. For them he was "cosmopolitan" – by that they meant Jewish – and that was enough.

With his high forehead and his waving hair brushed back, Fischer was brimming with intellectual energy and, despite his pale complexion, he looked younger than his fifty-five years. Conversation turned to Čapek. Oswald loved to play the part of the roving reporter, ferreting for details, and he ostentatiously took a notebook and pencil out of his pocket. "Mr Fischer, could you possibly give us your view of Germany's protest against the new film?"

Fischer laughed out loud. He had no intention of being diplomatic. Adopting a look of great seriousness, to reflect Oswald's own bit of theatre, he replied in his role as an official representative of Czech culture. "Let me put it this way. *White Disease* is a moral appeal." "Like all Čapek's work," Oswald cut in.

"Yes, but in this play he has dropped his old conciliatory tone. He is raising his voice against a spreading barbaric spiritual epidemic. He is crying out to the world that the supreme right of man is the right to live. It's actually quite simple."

"That's all well and good," Oswald frowned, "but in some of the papers they're saying that the very fact it's being played in the National Theatre is a provocation. It's full of class hatred and crude caricatures of today's Germany."

Oswald had read all the reviews and was genuinely interested to know what Fischer and Jelínek thought. A lively discussion followed. The waiter brought another bottle of the rich Slovak red for which the cellar was known. With my cheeks glowing I joined in the conversation, praising Zdeněk Štěpánek in the role of the General. Jelínek found him a bit affected and was more impressed by Hugo Haas as the dejected Galén.

"His pessimism is infectious," Jelínek mimicked Galén's gestures and gloomy tone. "So is his naivety …

"… or rather Čapek's naivety."

"But isn't Doctor Galén an extremist in himself, a kind of pacifist extortionist?" I was quickly realising what a good journalist Oswald was, needling out answers with provocative questions. He went on. "Galén's a utopian idealist, holding everyone to ransom. He's dangerous because he refuses to be pragmatic, to reach a deal with the General to prevent war."

"But aren't there times when that is just what is needed?" Jelínek replied. "Isn't Czechoslovakia just the same? Justified in defending herself by any means – even extortion – if she can't match the military might of the aggressor? Should the doctor make compromises with the General, when he knows the General's policies are leading everyone to annihilation? All I can say is – what a pity we don't have Galén's serum … "

Fischer smiled. "There, Mr Bamborough, Mr Jelínek has answered your question for me."

"It seems to me that he just added some more questions … "

"On the whole I prefer questions to answers." Fischer wound up the little interview. "Answers rule out other answers – and they're usually wrong."

The wine continued to flow and the conversation went on until morning.

Two days later Hitler's troops entered Austria.

And We Are Lost

In my dark little room in the shadow of Petřín Hill, I tuned into the international stations on shortwave, huddling by the wireless set, as if it might offer a little more warmth than the pale sun outside. Reception of the Reichssender from Berlin was excellent. As I listened, I looked down into the courtyard and watched my neighbour, paní Lašková, bent double, walking with her slop bucket filled to the brim as she crossed the little courtyard, putting the bucket down at every step. The Germans' English service was reporting on the Führer's triumphant appearance on the Heldenplatz in Vienna. His voice echoed round the courtyard, leaving the ancient, flaking walls and paní Lašková unmoved. Later I tuned to the Americans, being relayed on shortwave to Europe. There was a programme of Saint Louis Blues, that seemed almost as incongruous as the Führer. And then the familiar voice of the CBC anchor, Bob Trout, came on air …

> *Tonight the world trembles, torn by conflicting forces. Throughout this day, event has crowded upon event in tumultuous Austria. Meanwhile the outside world, gravely shaken by the Austrian crisis, moves cautiously through a maze of diplomatic perils …*

What followed, coming loud and clear through the crackles of shortwave was something I had never heard before. The broadcast included live pickups from London, Paris and other European cities, with comments on the latest developments. It was as if the world had shrunk to a fraction of its size. I could hardly believe that it was possible to bring together so many voices from so many different corners of the world. "The world has come to our little courtyard," I called down to paní Lašková. Some of the voices were faint, interrupted by static, but nearly everything could be made out. This was radio at its most vivid, and most vivid of all was a young reporter I was hearing for the first time, Edward R. Murrow, who was in Vienna. While the other presenters sometimes sounded over-excited, as if reporting on a ball game, he seemed to cut to the heart of what was going on. In a few sentences, he made quite clear the bleak future faced by the Jewish people of Vienna.

> *It was called a bloodless conquest and in some ways it was. But I'd like to be able to forget the haunted look on the faces of those long lines of people outside the banks and travel offices. People trying to get away … I'd like to forget the sound of smashing glass as the Jewish shops were raided; the hoots and jeers at those forced to scrub the sidewalk …*

I was taken back to my childhood. I was about ten, chatting on the bus with Danny Silver, a boy of roughly the same age, in our typical East End mixture of German, English and Yiddish. A well-dressed man sitting behind us interrupted our conversation, "If you're in our country, speak our language."

For a moment we were confused. I don't think we had even noticed the hybrid of a language we were speaking.

The man made himself clear. "You're making me uneasy, you orientals. In my own country. I don't know what you might be talking about."

I was quite at a loss, tears welling in my eyes. Danny took me by the arm and we hopped off as the bus slowed at the corner of Whitechapel Road. We went our separate ways without a word.

From then on, I always avoided catching Danny's eye at the bus stop, sometimes I would deliberately turn and wait around the corner if I saw him from a distance. We hardly spoke for several years and if our paths did cross I would say a curt hello in English and he would nod politely in reply. A wrong had been done and somehow I had made myself an accessory, out of nothing more than a foolish sense of embarrassment.

*

On Tuesday I went to the Café Juliš on Wenceslas Square, which always had the best selection of foreign papers in Prague. I sat in the plate glass window reading *The Times*, looking down occasionally on the flow of people on the wide pavements and the cars stopping and starting at the lights. The editorial gave confident reassurances that the Anschluss was nothing to worry about – all this was really no different from the English and the Scots coming together of their own free will all those centuries ago.

When I was very small, my mother used to read to me from Alice in Wonderland as I was going to sleep. At that moment I felt a bit like Alice.

"But I don't want to go among mad people," Alice remarked.

"Oh, you can't help that," said the Cat: "we're all mad here. I'm mad. You're mad."

"How do you know I'm mad?" said Alice.

"You must be," said the Cat, "or you wouldn't have come here."

I spoke three languages, but it felt as though words were turning into mere noises in all three, animal sounds that refer to nothing beyond themselves. What was I doing in Prague anyway? Suddenly, everything in the café seemed too big or too small, and for a moment I thought I was going to faint. I left the change in my pocket on the table and stepped out into the fresh air to let myself be swept along in the crowd to the top of the square. Before long I was at the radio headquarters in Fochova Street, a little out of breath, but more settled. I met Ivan Jelínek on the corridor. His face was pale and he hardly registered my presence. "Otokar Fischer is dead," was all he could bring himself to say. Fischer, who had been so very full of life at the National Theatre a few days earlier.

I followed Ivan to the studio. The story he told was, in miniature, the story of the tragedy of Austria. Fischer died with a peculiarly apt theatricality, at the moment he was being told of Hitler's occupation of the country. Ivan had written a hasty obituary; he could hardly control his voice as he began to speak into the microphone.

At the age of twenty-five, Otokar Fischer has passed away. He was being treated for a serious disease of the valves of the heart and as he was being told the news of the end of Austrian independence he suffered a massive heart attack.

Ivan had given Fischer's age as twenty-five instead of fifty-five. When I thought about it, the slip came as no surprise. It was exactly his own age and I knew that Fischer had been a role model to him, a kindred spirit. He recited two of Fischer's poems and at the end an extract from Goethe's poem *Limits of Mankind* in Fischer's beautiful concise translation.

Nás vlna zvedne
Nás pohltí vlna
A my jsme byli.

A few days before, Henlein's local party boss in Jägerndorf, a thug called Josef Barwig, had asserted that the Sudeten Germans had no interest in the Germany of Schiller and Goethe. Their cultural bond was with the Germany of Adolf Hitler. At the time we had laughed at his grotesque barbarism, but his dream was coming true.

That evening, with Fischer's translation in my mind, I tried to render the last lines of the poem into English.

The wave lifts us ... It drags us down ... And we are lost.

My English was inadequate and prosaic. But at least it was simple and clear, as befits the interpreter, and I felt a little better.

Easter Messages

With just a few days left till Easter, Parliament was in session for the last time before the break. In the Rudolfinum, the atmosphere was tense. I was interpreting for a handful of English-speaking journalists. The deputies for the Sudeten German Party were glowing with the confidence that the Anschluss had given them. "In the last few weeks, the great German nation has undertaken actions to change the course of world history ..." The party's parliamentary leader Ernst Kundt was soaring. "And it is with a proud awareness that they belong to this nation that the Sudeten Germans in recent days have at last overcome the fragmentation of their forces." He listed all the smaller Sudeten German parties that had agreed to come under the Sudeten German Party's umbrella.

Kundt was one of the cleverest politicians in Henlein's party. Most of the British journalists already knew him because he spoke good English and as a lawyer he knew how to articulate the ideas of his party with precision, without the strident excesses of some of his party colleagues. He went on, talking in the carefully weighed language of his lawyer's training about basic rights and justified demands. But his words were marching, not flowing. I tried to translate accurately. Kundt said that the newly united Sudeten Germans would from now on be in *closed ranks*. It was more than just a metaphor. These were the *tightly closed ranks* of the Nazi marching songs. My English colleagues, who were studiously taking notes and nodding from time to time, would not have picked up the reference. Kundt's speech ended with an assault on the Sudeten German Social Democrats and Communists. Just as on my visit to the borderlands a few weeks before, I had the unnerving feeling that Hitler's revolution had already reached us, even here in Prague, and was virtually complete.

Kundt was coming to the end of his speech: "The question as to whether the Sudeten German Party has the right to speak for all Sudeten Germans has today become quite clear, both at home and abroad. For anyone to ignore this reality is no longer possible, tactical or practical."

Czech deputies responded in various ways. Some made the point that the borders of Bohemia and Moravia had changed little for centuries, but their arguments had been repeated so often that they sounded tired, a memory rather than a reality. One deputy quoted the constitution, "We have given them more than was required of us in the peace treaties and in the constitution itself. We want nothing more from our Germans than loyalty to our Czechoslovak state."

A Sudeten German deputy cried out from the opposition benches in protest. "*Our* Germans! *Our* Germans! All the time you're talking about what you've given us. Will you never realise that what you so generously give us is nothing more than what you have stolen from us? The constitution isn't worth the paper it's written on if it only serves one side!"

Cries from across the chamber. The deputy speaker interrupted the debate, repeatedly ringing the division bell on the desk before him. It was several minutes before there was a semblance of order.

The debate went on. A government bill was being discussed, proposing an increase in the defence budget following the latest developments in Germany. The finance minister stood up and read off the costs involved. With the events in Austria, the danger of war seemed real enough. The chamber was tense to breaking point as the Sudeten German deputy Gustav Peters took the floor. He was one of Henlein's main economic advisers and in the last couple of years had been working vigorously to redirect industry and trade in the borderlands towards the Reich. As he spoke, he was carried on a wave of cheers from his party colleagues. His tone was one of deep sarcasm, "I have no choice but to state that the finance minister has succumbed to a *disease* ... a disease which appears to have become rather fashionable among members of our government, a disease which leads to each and every one of them taking on the mantle of minister of propaganda."

There was an explosion of laughter from the Czech benches. Someone shouted, "Ha! You've got it quite the wrong way around. You mean Herr Goebbels' little rash ... his *white disease*! We've no plans to share his bed, thank you very much!"

Another wave of laughter. Peters was not put off. "It is outrageous that the party of the finance minister is providing us with figures without in any way proving their accuracy. All this false information can only have one goal: to fan the mood in the streets of Prague and the Czech nation in general that will lead to their mobilisation against the Sudeten Germans. I can see no other reason for it."

This time there was loud applause from his fellow Sudeten German Party deputies. Peters stared menacingly across the chamber. "The latest developments in the German camp would be a warning to you, if only you had your ears open to such warnings. I can conclude with just one thing. Gentlemen, as a citizen of Prague I can tell you that you have done so much to cultivate the mistrust of Germans in the countryside, that you have lost them for good."

During the break I found myself in the queue for coffee next to a square-built man, whom I guessed to be in his mid-forties. He turned and introduced himself as Gustav Beuer. He was a Sudeten German Communist deputy, and I quickly realised that I was talking to a highly articulate and tough politician. I suppose he had to be tough in the face of Henlein's men who despised the Sudeten Communists and Social Democrats even more than they did the Czechs. He invited me to come to Liberec during the campaign for the May elections. Over a cigarette and Turkish coffee, he offered some wry insights, summing up the debate. "You need a strong stomach for this. The Czechs with their self-righteous cries of 'Today belongs to us!' and then Henlein's thugs sneering 'But tomorrow is ours!' You can almost see the uniforms under their suits. And, of course, they are right. Tomorrow really will be theirs, to all intents and purposes it already is, but none of that is thanks to their powers of persuasion. It's grotesque, their little pretence at being democrats. Come to North Bohemia and see for yourself."

"I shall be more than glad to accept your invitation," I assured him.

*

"The peace of all stems from the peace of the individual... and the peace of the individual stems from the peace of all ..."

A week had gone by and I was back in the parliamentary press gallery, high above the debating chamber. The voice was thin but clear; its owner looked austere, academic, although her face broke from time to time, as if by accident, into a nervous smile that was warm, almost childlike. It was Alice Masaryk, the daughter of Czechoslovakia's founding president. She was addressing the chamber, as she did every year on Easter Saturday, to declare the Easter Truce of the Czechoslovak Red Cross. Her words had nothing – nothing at all – in common with the debates we had been hearing in this same chamber a few days earlier. None of the Sudeten German politicians who had spoken then were present.

"Beautiful is this land of ours. Great are our possibilities in the real human culture, the culture which respects every immortal soul."

Her voice was a little higher and more fragile than I remembered it, or perhaps it was just the impression given by the oversized chamber. The parliament building, the Rudolfinum, had originally been built as a concert hall and its rather frivolous neo-Pompeian interiors seemed even more incongruous now than they had a week before. This was a building that spoke from a less troubled past.

Speaking slowly and deliberately, Alice Masaryk appealed to the newspapers, whatever their hue, to suspend, at least for a few days, their political battles. But as she begged us to try to *live in the truth*, I was no longer even sure what the words meant. They seemed as out of time as the Pompeian swirls on the ceiling above us.

Preaching to the converted and the unconvertable, was how Jelínek put it the next day, when Alice Masaryk came to the radio headquarters to read the speech again. With the help of his contacts abroad, Jelínek had achieved something of a coup. The American CBS network was to broadcast an English version on all its affiliated stations. "Coast to coast!" Jelínek declaimed in English, imitating the American radiomen with whom he had been negotiating. English was Alice Masaryk's second mother tongue, thanks to her American mother Charlotte.

Around two o'clock that night the speech was broadcast on shortwave, to time with the early evening audience on the American East Coast, and I listened from home. Masaryk's words would appeal to listeners in America. I lay on my bed, listening carefully and mapping the cracks on the ceiling. In English and without the distraction of the chamber, I could follow her ideas more clearly. She no longer sounded naïve and distant. I noted how she returned repeatedly to the idea of truth and freedom being tied to the responsibility borne by the individual, by *"every immortal soul"*. To an audience here in Europe, where the individual was becoming submerged in the mass, her appeal would meet with little understanding. Individual responsibility was becoming a symptom of weakness. I continued to look up at the ceiling for a long time after the speech had ended; the cracks were little roads in a pale, sunless desert, leading nowhere in particular.

*

On the way to the Deutsches Haus I was almost knocked down by my fellow countrywoman, the journalist Shiela Grant Duff.

She was turning the corner of Wenceslas Square and into Na Příkopě at a pace that was almost a run. I blushed and muttered an apology. "No, it was quite my fault," she insisted, "I expect we're heading for the same place." She hurried on with her mane of blond hair struggling to keep up with her. The Sudeten German Party had just published Henlein's "Carlsbad Programme", the latest list of demands, and was holding a press conference at the party headquarters. No sign of an Easter truce here.

I did not know Shiela well. I was a little intimidated by her striking good looks and self-confidence. Rather like Edgar Young, Shiela was an aristocratic rebel and she already had a reputation in Britain as a champion of the Czech cause. Her family was close to Churchill, related by marriage. Now Shiela was ploughing through the crowds on Na Příkopě, determined and decidedly Churchillian. I abandoned trying to keep up.

We found the party press department well prepared, with a neatly printed summary of their demands in German, Czech and in perfect English and French translations. Henlein's people had become adept at using the language of the western democrats to their own ends. They would speak of self-determination and the rights of nations as a justification for Germany and Hungary's territorial ambitions. Even in Britain and the United States, Shiela told me, everyone had begun talking about putting right the wrongs of Versailles. It all sounded very reasonable. The Carlsbad Programme was very much in this spirit.

Over coffee brought by an inscrutable German waiter, Shiela and I read through the points several times:

"It's strange, isn't it? The list sounds almost reasonable until you get to that last, eighth point, and try to decipher what it

55

might really mean." She slammed down her cup like a judge with his gavel and block, and I was surprised the cup didn't shatter. The waiter turned to us briefly and looked away. No expression crossed his face.

"Look … here it is. A call for *complete freedom to profess adherence to the German element and to German ideology.* What does that actually mean? *The German element... German ideology…* Here it might seem meaningless, but I spent several years living in Hitler's Germany, in the closed world of the revolution that Goebbels has cultivated so carefully. It is quite simple and logical … And, of course, it's also quite dotty."

I couldn't help smiling at her choice of a word that seemed to come so much from her old world of nannies and boarding schools. She noticed my smile, but if she was offended, she did not show it and carried on.

"Theirs is an ideology that excludes not only any other view of the world, but also its very right to exist." She looked up to me as she added. "And, of course, the right to exist of the person holding that view."

She returned to the text. "Look at the second point here. It says the Sudeten Germans should be declared a *legal personality*. That means the setting up of a Sudeten Diet and pushing through the Nationality Statute that Prime Minister Hodža has promised. Combine that with the eighth point, and it's quite simple."

Her tone was that of a prosecuting lawyer, slicing through the arguments of the defence.

"The Henlein party will do all it can to install National Socialist type institutions within the areas it controls – following the principle of the *German ideology.* Heaven help any German who is Jewish, Socialist or Communist. The German majority shall deal with the German minority as it sees fit. If you're in any doubt about what that means, have a look at what's going on across the border. And that's before we even begin to talk about the Czechs in the German majority areas."

And there Shiela rested her case. We chatted for a while over a glass of something a bit stronger than coffee and then she hurried off to pack her bags – "Being well connected has its advantages." She smiled broadly. "I'm off on a flying visit back to England. I've been invited to dinner with Churchill at Chartwell. It's rather well timed. I'd like to have a few words with him about all this. He won't get much of the story from Mr Chamberlain."

Poisoned Waves

The British journalists were keeping me busy. Bill Morrell, the *Daily Express*'s man in Prague, asked me if I would be willing to travel with him to the Sudetenland. Remembering Gustav Beuer's invitation I quickly arranged for us to go to Liberec. The local elections were only three weeks away and in the German-speaking areas everyone was predicting an overwhelming victory for Henlein. Morrell was a fair bit older than me, already a respected and well-established reporter, and there was more than a bit of the adventurer in him. He hated covering stories from the lounges of correspondents' hotels, where lazy reporters would pass rumours back and forth until they became facts. His fox terrier Pop rarely left his side.

In the car Morrell asked me about quirks of the Czech language and I told him what I knew about Czech history and legend. He was particularly taken by the story of the knights, waiting in Blaník Mountain to ride out in the nation's moment of greatest need, led by Saint Wenceslas himself. "I have a nasty suspicion," he noted, "that Czechoslovakia's foreign policy is relying a bit too much on that one."

My own story interested him too and he said he was looking forward to visiting me in London when all this was over. I think he found it refreshing that I was so young and that I wasn't a journalist. As Pop slept with one eye half open on the back seat I wondered whether Morrell had something of the terrier in him too. In any case, he would make a good match to Shiela Grant Duff, the Churchillian bulldog.

We parked on the square and Morrell walked around to let Pop stretch his legs. Man and dog both seemed in search of adventure. Many of the people in the streets were wearing the brown Sudeten German Party uniform and white stockings. Beuer shook hands with Morrell and greeted me warmly as we met outside the town hall. "We are well protected here," Beuer laughed, pointing up to the bronze statue of the Carolingian knight Roland which capped the tower. Liberec, or Reichenberg, as it was known to its German-speaking inhabitants, was a handsome town, and the town hall, an extravagant piece of Viennese neo-Gothic, looked rather out of place in the hills of North Bohemia. Two youths were watching our every move from behind a lamp post, clearly relishing their little game of espionage.

"Henlein's people monitor all my meetings," Beuer said apologetically. "They are preparing long lists of Jews and Bolsheviks for the Führer."

One of the young men pointed his small box camera at us. It looked just like the sturdy Zeiss Ikon I had bought myself with my first wages a few years before. "It's not just people like me they bully. They love to hang around outside Jewish and Czech-owned shops, noting down the names of Germans who dare to break Henlein's boycott. We all know each other here."

We went into the Café Post, which was a bastion of old world gentility with its high ceiling and Art-Nouveau stucco work, not quite Vienna, perhaps, but quite evidently aspiring. The hum of conversation mingled with the sound of the radio in the background. This was clearly not a place where the Communist Beuer would usually choose to spend an afternoon. He certainly would not succeed in canvassing many votes here. He explained that he had chosen the café because of another appointment, and a few minutes later a woman who I guessed to be in her mid-thirties joined us. As she swept between the tables, all eyes in the café looked up and followed her to her seat. Her hair was short, she was wearing loose-fitting men's trousers and a linen jacket, and her broad smile came almost as a shock in this subdued place. She shook our hands enthusiastically, "Milena Jesenská." I recognised her name immediately. She had written some of the best articles I had come across about the Sudetenland and Beuer told Morrell in his broken English that if there was anyone here who really understood the current crisis, she was that person. As we sat waiting to be served, the radio, the Reichssender Breslau, filled any moments of silence. It seemed to steer the conversation.

"You know, radio is just the same as the printing press at the time of the Reformation." Jesenská's tone was one of frustration rather than admiration. She pointed to the big Bakelite wireless in the corner, with its dial glowing orange like an open fire. "Gutenberg's invention meant that people could have their own Bible at home."

"Provided they were lucky enough to have been taught to read." The Marxist Beuer liked to get things right when it came to historical details.

Jesenská went on, "Today, thanks to radio, everyone can enjoy a concert at home in their kitchen, or a sporting event … and hear the latest news."

"If they can afford a radio," Beuer added from behind a cloud of smoke, but was quickly interrupted.

"… or if they spend time in their local pub or sports club."

She nodded towards the radio in the corner.

"For the last five years all the people in this part of the country have had to do is to turn a switch and Nazi ideology from the German radio stations has leaked unseen but not unheard into their living rooms. Of course they listened. It was in their language. We can hardly blame them for tuning to stations that they can understand." She was looking at Morrell, but never once gave the impression that she was trying to give the visiting Englishman a lesson. "And what have we done about it in Prague? We've given them half an hour a day in German. I'm not exaggerating … that's all you'll hear in German from Radiojournal. And you wouldn't believe how boring it is. By now people in the Sudetenland have been thoroughly re-educated, persuaded and bullied by what they hear from across the border. They are perfectly trained in parroting all those nice phrases about their right to self-rule and a national space. Just have a look at the pages of *Die Zeit*."

At this, she tossed aside the copy of the Sudeten German Party paper that she had been waving as she spoke.

"But Radiojournal is just expanding its German broadcasts," I ventured cautiously. "A whole new station is due to start next month from the transmitter in Mělník. You've heard about Prag II."

Jesenská picked up the paper again.

"Just have a look and see if you can find anything about it in there! Henlein has called on everyone, even the orchestras and dance bands, to boycott the station. And most are happy to oblige. I was talking to someone from the Teplitzer Musikverein only yesterday. I'm sure that Comrade Gustav here will confirm the picture."

She used the term comrade without irony. Although her paper *Přítomnost* was far from being left wing, Jesenská, like Beuer, was a socialist. They were on first-name terms and they shared a directness and energy that seemed to enthral Morrell, as he sat taking notes. The conversation between the two of them went back and forth from German to Czech and where necessary I translated for Morrell. The waiter walked by twice, ignoring us.

"It's even worse than Milena says," Beuer was in no mood for optimism. "Since the occupation of Austria, the Sudeten German Party leaders have created a situation that borders on anarchy. I'm not sure they even realise it in Prague. These people are using the crudest and most slanderous forms of propaganda and they've adopted all the Nazis' methods of exerting pressure, from spreading false alarm to open terror, to stir the people up into a constant fever, to deceive them and intimidate them."

Beuer looked across to the next table, from where we were being observed by the same boys we had seen half an hour earlier on the square. In the fin de siècle café, doing its very best to convince us that the last three troubled decades had never happened, they looked even more out of place than Beuer himself. The waiter brought them beer although they hardly looked old enough to be drinking alcohol, and then he walked back in a broad and awkward arc around our table towards the kitchen. The boys looked sheepish, self-conscious and Jesenská gave them a long disapproving glare. It would have been nice to think of them as a harmless irritation.

Beuer went on. "I could give you long lists of their intimidation techniques. The outcome is that people have the feeling now that they are actually living in the German Reich, that there's nothing left to decide. The party's public meetings, the shameless agitation, the endless marching to the sound of church bells … *church bells*, would you believe it … festooning public buildings with their banners. And then there's this … "

He was silent for a moment. The radio in the background continued: someone was talking about the new order in Austria. Beuer drew on his cigarette and inhaled deeply …

"… the broadcasts from the Reich. They are infecting hundreds and thousands of people every day. Radio has turned them into fanatics, who know only too well that the declarations by their party leaders about respecting the territorial integrity of Czechoslovakia are nothing but lies and smokescreens and that the real policies of the Sudeten German Party are what they hear four times a day in the news bulletins of the German wireless. That message, I can assure you, is clear and simple."

Beuer stopped, as if waiting for an answer. For a while Jesenská was silent and I had the impression she was reflecting on this last point. Then she said, "You could say that people are living in two places at once."

"That's just it."

I realised that Beuer was right. Sudeten German Party politicians talked about justice, autonomy, a second Switzerland, while their paymasters supplied a constant undercurrent of mistrust, hatred and fear. Radio was penetrating every corner of the Sudetenland. As we were speaking, as if on cue, the Reichssender had gone over to a speech from Vienna by Josef Bürckel, the man Hitler had appointed as Reichskommissar for the union of Austria with the German Reich. With that peculiar gun-toting reasonableness that the Nazis had become so good at, he was outlining how Beneš had forced the Slovaks and three-and-a-half million Germans into his Czech state. He had promised autonomy, but *of course* a man like that could never be trusted to keep any promise. And Bürckel concluded with an assurance that this would no longer be tolerated.

Were we on the brink of war? One of the things that had brought us to Liberec was to find out just how far Sudeten Germans had been sucked into the world of Goebbels' dream. I realised that to all intents and purposes they were already in the Reich.

In the end, we left without being served. I couldn't help thinking that if the café itself had had a voice, it would have disapproved strongly of such shabby treatment of customers.

"The waiter used to be in our party," Beuer pointed out. "I've known him all his life. If he served us, he could lose his job. He joined the Nazis after the Anschluss. The café owner is a party official. This is a state within a state. And where are the Czechs? Are they afraid? Do they think that this is all simply a German matter? That it's up to the Germans themselves to decide who they want to vote for? Or have they decided that you can only negotiate with those who have the real power? Prime Minister Hodža really does seem to prefer talking to Henlein than to us or the Social Democrats."

We spent the night at the hotel Zum Goldenen Löwen. The moment we walked in, Morrell's fox terrier got into a scrap with the dachshund of a German forester. I nervously imagined the diplomatic incident about to unfold, but the jovial forester laughed and bought the English guest a beer in the hotel bar. We're in good company, I thought to myself. The Führer is a dog-lover too. We exchanged greetings with the same man the next day, at Henlein's big Mayday rally.

*

Konrad Henlein was the man that everyone was talking about, and now I had a chance to see him. I had expected someone with extraordinary charisma and great rhetorical skill, and my expectations rose with the trumpet fanfare that introduced him. But he had neither.

Perhaps this was what made the rally so mesmerizing, the willingness of the crowd to be hypnotised by something that was simply in the air, an idea, a shared dream. There was something remarkably average about Henlein. He was neither small nor tall and he had the same round glasses as Beneš, making him seem harmless, a schoolteacher, a headmaster perhaps, at an important school event. And he lacked the oratorical skills of his master across the border. This didn't seem to matter. He raised his right arm, clenched his fist, and shook it violently in the air. I saw that Morrell was noting his every movement, his eyes moving back and forwards from Henlein to the crowd, from the fly to the fish. Henlein's voice rose in a paroxysm of furious oratory. *"Sieg Heil! Sieg Heil! Sieg Heil! Sieg Heil!"*

the crowd replied obediently. We were standing a little above Henlein and, stretching my neck, I could just see the paper from which he was reading. I could see that he was not improvising. Each word of the speech was written down, with thick black lines and other marks drawn under certain passages. As he reached the end of these passages he would raise his head, his right fist would go up and he would rise to a roar.

At one point I heard Morrell burst out laughing. I looked around, worried that someone might notice. He leaned towards my ear. "It's just the same rhythm as my old gym teacher, as he marched us round and round, barking out 'Left-right! Left-right! Left-right!' But this lot doesn't even need reminding. All their marching and sieg-heiling is already in perfect step."

Morrell's observations about Henlein's gymnastics made me laugh, but I was disturbed by what I had seen. I felt drained and was longing to get back to Prague, but Morrell was not so easily worn down. We took a lengthy detour to Carlsbad. We would just have time to see the Sudeten German Social Democrat leader Wenzel Jaksch address his own party's gathering.

Morrell drove and I slept for most of the way, but when I woke up just before we arrived, I was little refreshed. In Carlsbad we passed elegant hotels with landaus going back to the time of Edward VII. "They're waiting patiently for the clocks to turn back thirty years," Morrell chuckled. The road went on and we stopped on a piece of waste ground, where a crowd of about two thousand had gathered. With their loose brown jackets and dumpy brown caps, they looked very different from the crowd we had seen just a couple of hours before in Liberec. Their cries of *"Freiheit"*, sporadic and arrhythmic, were far from the waves of sound created by the crowds of Henlein's people. One group of workers from Bodenbach had just been dismissed from their factory for failing to join the Henlein demonstrations. These people were the real losers in this grim business. "They are a minority within a minority," Morrell observed, "and if one group in the Sudetenland is really being treated badly, here they are."

In the car, as we drove back to Prague as the long spring evening turned to night, Morrell worked up his notes. As the lights of the city approached, he read what he had written by torchlight, comparing Henlein and Jaksch.

The speaker was Wenzel Jaksch, their leader. He is a thin, pale, frail-looking man. He, too, gestured as he spoke, but not as much as Henlein did. He was a much better speaker than Henlein, but he was fighting a losing battle.

Henlein spoke on a platform, to which he had marched through an aisle of guards. He spoke in an open-air stadium, whose boundaries were draped with flags; a microphone spread his voice through loudspeakers. Behind him was a field telephone system, over which officials arranged the route to his next meeting. Jaksch pushed his own way through the crowd and was lifted on to a brewer's dray. He scribbled notes for his speech on the back of an envelope. He had no microphone or loud-speakers. In any case the crowd was not large enough for that.

"We are the last Mohicans of German Socialism," said Jaksch, and he meant it.

Driving through the countryside between Carlsbad and Prague among the wires and poles of the hop gardens where the spring shoots were already growing fast, for over half the journey we were in areas lived in almost entirely by German-speakers. The neat cottages and Baroque churches in the well-kept villages looked much the same in the Czech and German areas. Whatever this conflict was about, it was not a question of people who were irreconcilably different. They had just chosen to see themselves that way. Ideas of language and nation had twined themselves around them like the hop bines round the wires.

The next day, I met Shiela Grant Duff. She didn't mention her recent dinner at Chartwell, and I didn't press her for more. She too had just come back from the Sudetenland, driving her Škoda roadster through the Lusatian and Ore Mountains. Her stories were familiar. "You wouldn't believe it. Pictures of Henlein were framed in windows with evergreens and candles round them like icons. In Warnsdorf there was a bed which Henlein once slept in which had been carefully preserved in the condition in which he left it, even to the unchanged sheets. Quite dotty."

"Where do you think this is leading?"

"Czechoslovakia is falling apart from within, but it's not because the Czech gendarmes and soldiers couldn't keep order if they wanted. It's because they are under orders to do nothing."

I shrugged my shoulders, "But what could they do?"

"I don't know. Something. Their weakness is partly our fault. The British and French are urging the government to shut its eyes to all provocation, to govern with as light a hand as possible, to make every possible effort to avoid anything approaching an incident or anything which Germany could use as an excuse for attacking Czechoslovakia."

"But isn't it true that if Prague were to start ruling the border regions with a heavier hand, Hitler would send his troops straight in?"

"Then Prague can't win either way and it's up to us to help her."

The picture she was painting was of war. It seemed unimaginable that the quiet villages and towns where I had spent so much time in recent months could be transformed into a fratricidal battlefield.

"Oh yes, and I almost forgot. I've brought you something." She took a large cup, the traditional straight-sided Bohemian kind without a saucer, out of her leather satchel. "A present from Carlsbad." She laughed. "And by the way, did you know that Henlein is heading for London next week, a purely private visit, of course. He says he wants to correct the distorted image the British have of this whole business. One thing I do know is that he's asked for a meeting with Churchill. I'm sure he'll be charming enough, but I have given Churchill a bit of background, so I don't think he'll be deceived."

On one side of the cup was an image of Henlein in uniform, on the other, Hitler. And the words *"Unsere Hoffnung"* – our hope – running in Gothic script beneath them both.

The Owl

I was in Prague for the local elections three weeks later. Out of
habit, I got up and switched on the radio. As it warmed up with
its reassuring hum, I went out onto the little gallery which, as
in so many old Prague houses, went right round the courtyard
on each of the three floors. The late May air, flavoured with the
sweet pepper of acacia, filled the little room. Paní Lašková, bent
double, was fussing around in the courtyard, muttering to herself.
"What's the time?" she clucked as she spotted me. As always, not
waiting for an answer, she added, "Morning or evening?" and
bustled off towards the front gate with her slop bucket.

A familiar monotone came from the radio. I went back inside,
and recognised the high, thin voice of President Beneš. A partial
mobilisation. Germany, he declared, is massing troops on the
border.

I went straight to the main post office off Wenceslas Square
and phoned through, after several attempts, to an English-
woman I knew who was now living in Berlin. Margaret Koller
was an interpreter, married to a German schoolteacher and they
had two small children. She sounded nervous and I felt awkward; it was clear that she was not sure what she should say on

the telephone. Berlin, she said, was rife with rumours that the British were about to launch air raids, should German troops cross into Czechoslovakia. They had their car packed up and were ready to leave the city at any moment.

I walked out into the street. Loudspeakers were relaying instructions for reservists to join their battalions.

Something like this had been in the air for a long time, but still I found it hard to believe. Just around the corner was the Hotel Ambassador, where I found Morrell. We must go to the borderlands to see for ourselves. Quickly I sorted out a car and ran back home to throw a few clothes into my weekend case.

And then it was all over. The mobilisation orders were withdrawn. Radiojournal's broadcasts appealed for calm, repeating every half hour that war was not about to break out and that German troops had withdrawn from the border. Exactly what had happened remained a mystery, but for the Sudeten German Party it was clear. They immediately issued a statement about Czech provocation and lies, peppering it with stories of incidents with Czech gendarmes terrorising Sudeten German civilians.

A note arrived in the afternoon post from Oskar Ullrich, the Sudeten German Party spokesman. I was to come to the Deutsches Haus for breakfast at eight-thirty. Paní Lašková was haunting the little courtyard again. "Morning or evening?" I was reassured to see her. I filled a glass of water and collapsed onto the bed, feeling detached from the events around me. As I drank, I wondered if, like Alice in Wonderland, I would shrink to just ten inches tall.

I was almost surprised when I woke up, little refreshed but quite my normal size, to another balmy spring morning. I was glad for the walk across the Charles Bridge and through the Old Town to the broad avenue Na Příkopě. Most of the shops were still closed, here and there metal shutters were being pulled up, but the gate to the Deutsches Haus was wide open. In the gloom of the half-lit cloakroom I bumped into Eleanor Whitmore from United Press. She was crackling with dry wit as always. "So, you've been summoned by the owl too, have you?" she drawled. As we went up the broad steps leading to the dining room, Ullrich stood at the top, not so much an owl as an overweight bald eagle on his perch a flight above us. He took the big, round tortoiseshell-rimmed glasses out of his pocket, polished them with a handkerchief, dabbed his pate with the same handkerchief, and, by now looking rather more the owl, went into his usual routine. "Come on up the apples and pears," he giggled. During his years in London, selling Jablonec jewellery, Ullrich prided himself on having picked up Cockney rhyming slang, which he would use and abuse at every opportunity.

A couple of other journalists were already sitting in the dark, panelled restaurant. I saw Beuve-Méry from *Le Soir*, looking very uneasy as he sipped his coffee. Eleanor Whitmore's husband Bill was there too; he threw a casual half-nod to his estranged wife, settled back to his paper and downed a schnapps with his coffee.

Ullrich handed us all an account of the latest atrocities, perfectly produced at extraordinarily short notice. *Greueltaten*, was the German word that came into my mind as I tried in my head to translate Ullrich's carefully crafted English back into German. The word is so much more vivid than mere "atrocities". On Friday night, a Czech policeman had opened fire, unprovoked, on two Sudeten Germans on a motorcycle. "There is no evidence, not one shred, that they failed to stop when challenged by the policeman." Ullrich went on to quote a witness and circled the table theatrically, like a schoolmaster teaching a long-rehearsed lesson. "The Führer has demanded that the two victims be given a public funeral with full military honours. The British prime minister has been informed of this act of state terrorism." He stressed these last two words with relish and called on the waiter to bring another round of schnapps.

"To our martyrs!" He raised his glass. Some of the journalists absentmindedly stopped taking notes and raised their glasses too. I read the further details: the time, the place, the demand that the Czechoslovak Foreign Minister initiate a thorough investigation. I made my apologies and got up to leave. Despite myself I downed a schnapps and headed out, though not before he had warmly shaken my hand. Eleanor Whitmore had made her getaway more stealthily. "Do thank her for me," Ullrich said politely.

Since the mobilisation crisis, I had felt permanently uneasy. I knew Ullrich's stories would make it to the wires and would earn a paragraph in papers around the world, but I had no idea how true they were. I didn't even bother calling round at the Czechoslovak ministry. It was Saturday, and no one would be there. Ullrich invariably summoned the press at the weekend. He knew that no one would manage to contact a Czech bureaucrat on a Saturday or Sunday. It drove Bill Morrell mad, "Czechs never stop explaining the historical reasons why Henlein's demands cannot be fulfilled," he complained over his beer, as I outlined the details of Ullrich's little press conference. "They defend their borders with the argument that they've been there for a thousand years. But at ten thirty in the evening, just as my day's work is beginning, and when the Sudeten German Party is declaring one clash after another in North Bohemia, you can guarantee that the gentlemen of the Czechoslovak state news service will be tucked up in bed."

"And the owl is nocturnal, always to be found, ready to feed his chicks with a juicy, quotable morsel."

"While the Foreign Ministry remains convinced that the true version of the incident can wait till morning."

"Truth will prevail!"

I was taken aback by the irony of my own words. I had changed in the last months.

It was slowly dawning on me that truth, for people like Ullrich, and for millions of other adherents to the German revolution, lay in the future. Present reality was just an unfortunate obstacle that would need to be removed. If the journalists were willing to play his game, so much the better.

For all the unrest, the local elections went ahead.

Pentecost

In the first round, Henlein won an overwhelming majority throughout the Sudetenland. But the greater surprise was that a fifth of the Sudeten German voters still had the courage to vote against him. In the days leading up to the second round, I decided to make another trip to the borderlands, this time on my own and to the countryside.

It was the morning of the first Sunday in June, when I found myself walking up the valley side to the old pilgrimage church in Wiese – Ves u Liberce in Czech. An aromatic, light breeze was licking the grass of the uncut meadows, and the rolling landscape was humming with bees, a hum rather like the sound of my radio when I switched it on each morning. I chuckled to myself and wondered whether I was more at home in Nezval's world of phonomotors and electric birds than in the Bohemian countryside.

A bell began to summon the congregation to Mass. How many generations of these families had gone through their lives punctuated by its slightly mournful sound? It must have survived the Great War, when nearly every church in Austria-Hungary had given up its bells to be melted down for King and

Emperor. Perhaps that had been one of Father Reichenberger's little miracles.

Emmanuel Josef Reichenberger was the parish priest. We had met a few weeks earlier, when he had been in Prague to record an Easter message for Radiojournal. He had an easy way with strangers and we had become friends straight away. Our chat by the paternoster lift had ended with him extending an open invitation for me to come to his parish.

Reichenberger was a good friend of the Sudeten Social Democrat leader Wenzel Jaksch and, having spent over two decades working with the poor in the industrial areas in and around Liberec, had earned the nickname, the "Red Chaplain". He was rather an unlikely working-class hero, conservative and openly nostalgic for the old Habsburg Empire. Yet he and Jaksch had become comrades in arms, thrown together by a common enemy.

Mass was about to begin. Father Reichenberger beamed at me as he ducked and emerged through the little door of the sacristy, adjusting his vestments, red for the Feast of Pentecost. He spotted me immediately even with the church so crowded. I supposed that strangers were a rarity. He strode through to the back of the church and shook my hand enthusiastically.

I enjoyed the Mass. With the door open, I imagined how the organ and the singing must sound from the meadow outside. Father Reichenberger opened the old Bible on the lectern, surveying his congregation briefly before he began. He read very slowly and very deliberately:

*When the day of Pentecost had come, they were all together
in one place. And suddenly from heaven there came a sound
like the rush of a violent wind, and it filled the entire house
where they were sitting. Divided tongues, as of fire, appeared
among them, and a tongue rested on each of them. All of them
were filled with the Holy Spirit and began to speak in other
languages, as the Spirit gave them the ability.*

There was a long pause, long enough for some of the congregation to look up to the priest in expectation. There was emotion
in his voice, but I could see no change in his face:

*Now there were devout Jews from every nation under heaven
living in Jerusalem. And at this sound the crowd gathered and
was bewildered, because each one heard them speaking in the
native language of each. Amazed and astonished, they asked, 'Are
not all these who are speaking Galileans? And how is it that we
hear, each of us, in our own native language? Parthians, Medes,
Elamites, and residents of Mesopotamia, Judea and Cappadocia,
Pontus and Asia, Phrygia and Pamphylia, Egypt and the parts of
Libya belonging to Cyrene, and visitors from Rome, both Jews and
proselytes, Cretans and Arabs—in our own languages we hear
them speaking about God's deeds of power.' All were amazed and
perplexed, saying to one another, 'What does this mean?'*

The passage came back to me from childhood. I had always
loved that long list of hard-to-pronounce place names, the
idea of the bewildered crowd, so surprised and excited at suddenly understanding one another's languages. From Father
Reichenberger's mouth, the words from the New Testament

sounded like a direct challenge to his congregation, and an act of defiance.

In the porch after Mass I realised how poor many of these people were. They were in their Sunday best, but in the unforgiving bright spring sunshine I could see their clothes were patched and worn, especially the frocks and greasy leather shorts of the children. I was a little embarrassed: I was being paid well; my clothes were from the city, expensive, but hardly suitable for Sunday Mass.

An old widow in a black headscarf came up to Father Reichenberger. "They say the Führer is not a believer," she said rather hesitantly, addressing me but turning to the priest, "but I know he is a good Christian, like our Father Emmanuel here." Sharply and awkwardly, she turned away, and I had the feeling that whatever else she wanted to say had caught in her throat. As we walked down to the presbytery Father Emmanuel smiled sadly, "These ideas of the German revolution … they do not come from our people, but people are beginning to believe that there is nothing else out there. They are being bullied and flattered by the German revolutionaries into seeing Hitler as the future. They do not trust Prague, which is no great surprise, and they are rapidly losing their faith in anything I have to offer,"

He looked back to the church, starkly white in the midday sun. "They talk about the nation, but the nation is not the primary value and it is certainly not the only value. The nation is something that God gives us and for which God makes us responsible." His words sounded like a sermon, but they were heard only by me and the bees of North Bohemia. "We cannot accept the deification of the nation and all those other things

80

that go with it – blood, soil, race. It's frightening to see how our people are changing." By now he was quite animated. It was clear that Father Reichenberger was glad to have someone to talk to about ideas that had been turning over in his mind. "You probably know that the Christian Social Party has merged with Henlein's people. At the time Father Hilgenreiner insisted that this did not mean they were embracing National Socialism. But I've just found an article he's written for *Die Zeit*…" At this point he pulled out yesterday's paper from a fold in his cassock and turned to the back page. "This is what he writes: '*The question which concerns us is not – are you a Catholic, a Protestant, a free thinker – but are you German? He who by blood and conviction answers this question in the affirmative recognises National Socialism.*' Even he is saying these things. Will it be me next? Or you? Where are these voices coming from?"

As we parted, Father Reichenberger put a book in my hand. It was a collection of stories in Czech by Richard Weiner. He smiled. "It's not my taste … *Not my cup of tea*," he added in English. "My niece left the book here. She's in Prague with her little boy. Would you mind giving it to her? She loves these modern things." He tore a corner from the newspaper and wrote her address. "She's called Ilse."

Not a Hint of Politics

One consequence of the May elections was that many Czech intellectuals realised with a shock just how little they knew their Sudeten German compatriots and how little they understood their grievances. The May crisis aroused an awful awareness that the country could be on the verge of civil war – Czechs, many with German names, fighting Germans with Czech names. It was Karel Čapek, who articulated this feeling most vividly. Not even the radio's overcautious programme director Kareš was able to say no, when Čapek asked to address German listeners through the new Prag II station in German.

My Dear German Listeners,

Every nation has its peculiarities, some bigger, some smaller. Take the Germans, for instance. Among many things, they are a writing nation. Every time one of my books or even just an article has been published in German translation, I have received more letters from our Sudeten areas and from the other side of our borders than from anywhere else. Sometimes they were objections, at other times words of agreement, sometimes they were trying to put me right on some point, at others they were like a hand outstretched in friendship. I almost envied German writers for having such readers and such contact with them, for contact with people, I mean real contact with real people, is one of life's most valuable gifts.

In return I am now turning to you. You see, I have something on my mind. Sometimes it seems as if Prague were further away from Žatec or Česká Lípa than from the antipodes of New Zealand. We seem to find it hard to understand one another. It is not a question of language. If you travel around the world, you can make yourself understood by a Dutchman, a Spaniard, even an Englishman, without understanding a single word of his language. With a bit of patience we can all make ourselves understood as long as we talk about simple things in life, understandable to all people, and as long as we have goodwill. There is no point reflecting on where goodwill can or cannot be found. We have to make the effort. I would like to propose that we put our goodwill to the test, as it were, person to person.

Nations cannot talk to each other directly, but people can. I am not just speaking for myself, but for all Czechs and Slovaks, who write and think. Perhaps we are perceived in some way as part of the Czechoslovak public conscience, and we would sincerely like to understand you, our German fellow citizens. What someone says in your name is not as important as what you yourselves have to say about your own lives, about your disappointments and hopes, about how you would like to imagine a better, freer, more humane world. We would like to hear from you as individuals, where you feel a grievance and on the other hand what you like in this country we share. Perhaps we could even go beyond this and speak in greater depth about

some of these things. I think that, at the very least, it would give
us both a sense that we have come to know each other a little
better as decent people and loyal neighbours. Even that would
be a huge gain for both sides.

Think about it: Is it worth a try? Or do you feel there is no
point in other people and other nations trying to understand
you at a human level? I am sure this is not the case, so please
write to us, telling us quite openly what is on your mind.
Address your letters to the German-language broadcasting
station – I give my assurance that they will not fall on deaf
ears. In the meantime, let me send you my best wishes, as one
of many people working in Czechoslovak culture, for whom, in
the spirit of Masaryk, love for our own nation does not mean
hatred toward other nations.

Listening in my little room in silence, but for the half-muted
clatters and mumbles of paní Lašková, which punctuated so
much of my life in that old house, I did not imagine that many
Sudeten Germans would listen.

I was proved wrong. Two days later, I found a note from Jelínek stuffed under my door. I must come into the radio. He had
news about Čapek's message. We met in the foyer and immediately he started to explain, "Čapek has received hundreds of
letters and they're still coming in." For a moment I must have
looked a bit confused. "From Sudeten Germans who heard the
broadcast. Some of them are aggressive, in the curt language
of their revolution, but most of them are factual and polite."
I was surprised. I had assumed that most Sudeten Germans
had become quite immune to anything a Czech liberal-thinking

writer might have to say to them. "I think it has something to do with the intimacy of radio," Jelínek suggested, "they must have really felt that he was talking to them."

I found out later that day that Čapek had asked to be given airtime to reply to the letters.

"That pathologically cautious Kareš says it is out of the question." Jelínek was referring to Radiojournal's programme director Miloš Kareš. "Who is he scared of offending? Henlein himself, perhaps? By all reports Čapek is furious. He promised to respond to people's letters, and that is just what he plans to do. He has taken the whole lot of them with him to his country house in Strž and apparently he is replying to them one by one."

*

There was a growing sense of rebellion among the journalists in Radiojournal. Jelínek and Disman were getting ever more frustrated by the habit of Czech politicians to see the radio as a battleground for their own political struggles. Parties would vie for influence on the airwaves, and this had left the radio management cautious and self-censoring, just in case they might get into trouble with one side or the other. While outside the radio building the country was being torn apart, inside there was an incongruous sense of business as usual.

So it came as something of a surprise when the radio director Šourek began talking about the need to cultivate, as he put it in a note to his editorial staff, "not only the idea of our state's democracy, but also a national awareness among our listeners." Perhaps that was why he turned a blind eye to some very obvious dissident activity breaking out.

Jelínek introduced me to Miloslav Disman, who, together with some of the best people at the radio – people like Očadlík, Kocourek and F.K. Zeman, all household names in Czechoslovakia – had set up a new programme: Okénko. The word meant "window" and the programme was conceived as a window onto Czechoslovak society. No politics, of course. Or so it seemed. I'd happened to hear one of its first editions, a report about the life of the Czech minority living in the German-speaking areas. It had ended with the words:

From Aš to Jasina our chorale of loyalty and love can be heard for this wide and lovely country. We are here and we shall remain. We are here and we shall not give up one inch of our free land.

"No politics at all," I laughed.

"Well, Mr Kareš is a little bit suspicious," Disman acknowledged with a Cheshire-Cat grin, "but we have to do something. It won't be coming through our news coverage. That's in the hands of the Czechoslovak News Agency, and that, in its turn, is in the hands of the farmers' party, and they are not willing to rock the boat. So instead we talk about – how shall I put it? – ordinary life in Czechoslovakia."

"From Aš to Jasina," Jelínek added, roaring with laughter. But he went on in a serious and almost business-like tone that I was hearing from him for the first time. "We want these programmes to be examples of real, modern radio, lively and about how people live their lives. The country is in danger, but where is our national awareness? It's not just the Germans and the Hungarians who are claiming that Czechoslovakia is a thing of the past. There are plenty of people here too – even right here in this building – who have already decided that if we face a choice between Russia and Germany, Hitler is the lesser evil."

I wanted to interrupt, but he pressed on.

"And there's something else. We are not looking beyond our borders. We should be shouting out to our allies for help."

With that he turned to me.

"We have to talk to the world outside, to France and the English-speaking countries. At least radio can give us an illusion of having friends out there. The Christmas broadcast should have been just the beginning. We need your help too. You're an Englishman." I detected no irony in Jelínek's smile.

And so it was. A few days later I was out in the streets with Miloslav Disman. The Okénko team had decided to make a whole series of special outside broadcasts to report on the international Sokol celebrations that were just about to start in Prague. The word *sokol* means "falcon" and the Sokol movement was all about physical training and mass gymnastics. I have to admit that I was less than enthusiastic, with memories from school of endless physical education classes in the damp, windswept yard, with a big pile of wet black coal in the corner.

Sokol had its roots in the Czech national revival in the 19th century, a time when patriotic sports clubs were popping up all over Europe. The movement had spread rapidly throughout the Slavic nations and beyond. In the Czech consciousness it was associated above all with the idea of the Czechoslovak state, with the country's founding father T.G. Masaryk and his daughter Alice. At the big Sokol gatherings, thousands of people would exercise to music, much of it composed especially for the event.

I was not alone in finding it all rather strange. We interviewed the Irish publisher Andrew Byrne who happened to be in Prague and asked him about his impressions of Sokol, which had completely taken over the city streets. The interview took an accidentally comic turn. The rather bookish Mr Byrne was in unfamiliar territory. "It's very … er … very … colourful," he said, his rich literary vocabulary abandoning him. "Those costumes we passed along the street strike the western visitor as rather highly … er … coloured, but … er … in time the eye accustoms itself to the high colouring and you get the details," Mr Byrne was beginning to warm up, "… the beautiful embroidery, the harmonisation of colouring, the manner in which the design of the clothing has been made to fit. All these things have been made to harmonise in such a way that you get … hm … the twentieth century against a Greek background." I found it hard to keep a straight face as I translated for Disman. To Mr Byrne's and my own relief, the conversation then turned to Czech-Hibernian literary relations, which had never been better.

People had come to the Sokol meeting from all over the world – Yugoslavia, Romania, North and South America. Many were of Czech or Slovak ancestry. For months, one Czech from Texas told me, first, second and third generation Czech Americans had been exercising in front of their radio sets, practising for the event by following instructions from Radiojournal's North American service. It seemed to have worked. Descendants of Czech settlers in Nebraska, who didn't speak a word of the language, joined in gymnastics displays with Czech farmers from Romania, who spoke in an archaic rural dialect that had long since died out back home. There was even a delegation of Czechs from Austria and it was a very odd sight to see them at this celebration of shared Slav identity marching under the Nazi swastika. Without it, Disman told me, they would not have been allowed to come. Only Poland and the Soviet Union were absent: Poland because of the lingering border dispute over the Těšín area, a dispute which Hitler was doing much to stoke, and the Soviet Union because all this was quite clearly nothing other than a blatant display of bourgeois nationalism.

The Radiojournal outside broadcasting vans were present at each event, with Disman standing on a podium rather like a carnival float, painted in the red, white and blue of the Czech tricolour. He stretched out the microphone on a pole in the bright sunshine to catch the sound of the celebrating crowds. He reminded me of a conductor with his baton or a magician with his wand.

As we watched through the big first-floor window of the Café Juliš on Wenceslas Square, the usually rather doleful American radio correspondent Maurice Hindus was overwhelmed. "The Germans can never conquer these people," he enthused. "The only way they can ever live in peace with each other is with democracy – on both sides of the frontier."

"Let's admit it," said Jelínek, back to his usual ironic tone, "our broadcasts are pure propaganda. We're President Beneš's brownshirts. Look, we've quite convinced Mr Hindus already."

There was something in what Jelínek said. Earlier that day, at the huge Strahov Stadium, the Czech infantry had put on a display, ten thousand men, spread out in files. Ten thousand bayonets pulled out of their sheaths, all in perfect time. The troops raised their rifles, paused, sweeping down and up, combined with a stamp, as they lunged forward at an imaginary enemy. There were no officers on the field to shout orders, the loud-speakers and the crowd were silent, but each soldier might have been a machine in the precision of his movements.

I had mixed feelings. This was all very foreign to me. Was this crowd a mass of the kind that Goebbels was creating in Germany? Was this just further evidence of the values of the new Germany seeping across the borders? Was Sokol any different from the German gymnastic clubs, the *Turnvereine*, that were doing so much to stir up nationalist and militarist sentiment among Germans on both sides of the border? In what ways and according to which rules can a nation show its strength at a time when its very existence is under threat?

One answer came from Karel Čapek a couple of days later in the paper *Lidové noviny*, where he wrote that in the "Valley of Tears of propaganda", the person who fails to give his country any chance of fighting it is no cleverer than he "who refuses to arm his state in a world of sabre-rattlers." This was not the pacifist Galén from *White Disease* speaking.

Radiojournal's new German language station Prag II broadcast reports in German from the Sokol gathering, but I wondered how many Sudeten Germans were actually listening to it all. Goebbels, as usual, was a step ahead. For many months, preparations had been under way for the huge Turn- und Sportfest in Breslau, the capital of German Silesia. This was to bring together German sportsmen and women from all over the Reich – but that was not all. It was also the biggest ever gathering of *Volksdeutsche*, Germans from beyond the country's borders. The Sudeten Germans were the guests of honour, and the former sports teacher Henlein was ecstatic. Ironically, he had attended the Sokol gathering in 1926, and ever since then he had well understood the potential of big sports events. Ten years later, Hitler had won Henlein's heart forever with an invitation to take a place of honour at the Berlin Olympics. The Sportfest in Breslau promised to be on an unprecedented scale.

I hastily contacted Oskar Ullrich, to try to gain accreditation. As always he was all smiles and efficiency, and everything was sorted out in a few hours. He even arranged a car to take several Prague-based journalists the 280 kilometres to the city. The chatty party official who drove us was excited, but his enthusiasm was nothing compared with the jubilant crowds we met in the streets as soon as we crossed the River Oder into the old town.

Breslau was decked out in flags. At first sight this was a mirror image of Sokol. People had come from across the world – there were delegations from Transylvania, Argentina, South West Africa. There were cheerful crowds everywhere, the folk costumes looked quaintly old-fashioned against the old houses of the Ring. But the swastikas did not. And they were everywhere.

An endless column of athletes passed Schweidnitzerstrasse, marching in perfect time. They were the front of the huge delegation from the Sudeten Gymnastic Association. Goebbels had given away twenty thousand Sportfest tickets to Sudeten Germans and they made up by far the biggest group of Germans from beyond the Reich. I could just make out the Führer as the crowd drew level with him. This was the first time I had seen him, and although he was only a spot in the distance, a uniform among others, my heart missed a beat. He stepped forward, stood at the edge of the balustrade, raised his right arm and greeted the Sudeten German banners. The man standing next to me shouted ecstatically with the crowd, holding his hat, as if the wave of excitement were about to sweep it from his head.

Another huge roar. The Führer returned to his place and Konrad Henlein stepped forward.

> "Many thousands of German men and women, boys
> and girls from beyond the country's borders have come
> together here in Breslau for the greatest gathering of Germans from beyond the country's borders in the history
> of the Greater German Reich. Germans from all over the
> world, from all the different countries to which fate has
> carried our fellow Germans, have come together for a true
> German national celebration."

There was a mood of real joy. The flags and banners waved.

> "The German nation in the Reich has welcomed its brothers and sisters with open arms. Germans from overseas,
> from the former German colonies, our fellow Germans
> from all the German communities in Europe, and above all
> from countries bordering with Germany. At this moment
> it is a great honour in the name of Germans beyond Germany's frontiers, to express our immense gratitude for this
> opportunity. On this occasion the German spirit in our
> fatherland and the German spirit beyond its borders are
> united in a splendid and festive celebration."

I counted that Henlein had used the word "German" or "Germany" sixteen times in the first three sentences. The crowds were intoxicated.

"We, Germans from abroad, have an obligation to render unto the state that which is the state's and unto the nation that which is the nation's."

I couldn't help thinking about Father Reichenberger and what he would have made of this strange mutilation of the Gospel.

"We have become one nation, a united community of all the Germans in the world. A new German nation has come into being and a new German state. For us, Germans from beyond the Reich's borders, it is a festive and profound joy to behold the new Reich created by the Führer. We have come to Breslau as the grateful guests of the Reich."

For some reason an image I remembered seeing three months earlier in a run-down backstreet in Carlsbad came back to me, just a single image, like a still life. It was a poster, strikingly well designed, but torn and scribbled over, that I had seen peeling from a broken fence. The poster had advertised a workers' football tournament, organised by Jaksch's Social Democrats. I rather doubt the tournament even took place. In Henlein's sports clubs football was banned as un-German.

"We admire and welcome the great and living work that Adolf Hitler is carrying out for Germany. We, Germans abroad, are experiencing the work of the German revolution with a force and intensity, which people in Germany itself can scarcely imagine, because we know that the greatness and happiness of the Greater German Reich is the greatness and happiness of the whole German nation. We know too that the greatness and happiness of the Greater German Reich is the greatness and happiness of all Europe. It is our deepest conviction that it is the historical destiny of Germany to establish German justice among nations. That is the only thing that can bring real and permanent peace to our troubled part of the world. We owe our success in finding our deep inner unity to one man, Adolf Hitler ..."

The spectacle was electrifying. I could easily imagine all these young athletes going back to the Sudetenland the following week, their classrooms buzzing with the excitement of the adventure they had just been part of and the thrill of the promise of a glorious future, while the children of non-Nazis would be sitting in the corner, bitterly resenting their parents for making them stay at home and miss the fun, ostracised even by their teachers, almost all of whom had by now joined the Party.

*

I climbed the steep steps to the third floor of one of the brown-grey tenements almost in the shadow of the railway viaduct and knocked on the door. Karlín was Prague's first nineteenth century suburb and the most Dickensian part of the city, with factories, workshops, low workers' houses and blocks built with outside stairs and galleries around deep courtyards. In the courtyards there were often further workshops, and this particular yard was filled with steam from a laundry on the ground floor, with sheets put out to dry. It reminded me of the East End.

A three- or four-year-old curly-haired lad opened the door. When he saw an unfamiliar figure stooping over him, he ran out and hid behind a flowerpot that was much too small to hide him. A young woman, with her dark-blond hair cut short, appeared and asked what I wanted, cautious but not unfriendly. Mumbling something about Father Reichenberger, I held out Richard Weiner's stories rather awkwardly, like a passport to a border guard. She glanced at the book and her face lit up. Straight away I was invited in and once my eyes had got used to the darkness of the little room, I realised that it was filled from floor to ceiling with books. She put a pot on the coal-fired stove for coffee.

Ilse spoke about her uncle with affection. In fact he was not an uncle at all but an old family friend. He had looked after her when her parents were sick, and when they died he had taken her into his care. "I think he was a little in love with my mother, but he never let it show." She joked about his old-Austrian manners and Old Testament piety. "Well, did he like the book?" she asked, with feigned gravity.

"I think *modern* was the word he used." We laughed. Over coffee I told her about London, about our bit of the East End that was quite like Karlín. The idea of the Babel of languages and mix of religions and nationalities captured her imagination. "I shall come and see you one day. Do you promise you'll show me round?" I wrote my mother's address, which she slipped into a copy of Dickens' Great Expectations. "I won't lose it that way." Her little boy, Peter, listened closely, perhaps he sensed a future adventure.

We talked about the Sudetenland and I laughed when Ilse impersonated the Henlein followers, parodying the language they used and their endless marching. We both chuckled when I recounted Shiela Grant Duff's story about Henlein's bed. Peter laughed too.

We talked for many hours, long after Peter had been tucked up in his little plank bed in the corner. When I asked cautiously about Peter's father, she just shrugged, "It didn't work out." She asked about London again. She had just read the new Czech translation of Eliot's The Waste Land. "Is it true that there are eight million people living there?" She rummaged in a pile of books and dug it out in English, "... *so many/ I had not thought death had undone so many*. I can't imagine it. But it must be nice to be anonymous in the big city. I'm learning English from Eliot, but I'm not very far yet."

Unselfconsciously, she invited me to stay the night. We shared her small bed, our bodies scarcely touching. Half asleep I listened to the occasional hiss of the embers in the stove and to the faintest sound of Ilse and Peter breathing.

Party Uniforms

Neville Chamberlain's envoy, Lord Runciman was due in Prague the following week. In the Sudetenland, the arrival of the British delegation was awaited with some enthusiasm, Prague was a great deal more cautious, but courteous. I heard that President Beneš was lost for words and went red in the face when the British ambassador confronted him with the idea, but of course the president had no choice but to accept the delegation. Chamberlain's plan was that Runciman would mediate and find an answer to the *Czech question*.

Lord and Lady Runciman arrived at Prague's Wilson Station just before three in the afternoon on the 3rd of August. In the hot sunshine the retired businessman was looking tanned and relaxed as if he had come to see the sights. Later a member of the delegation let slip that Runciman had just returned from a few days' sailing, which explained his colour and perhaps why the pages of the book under his arm, Elizabeth Wiskemann's *Czechs and Germans*, were pristine and uncut. Lady Runciman was elegant and ebullient, clearly enjoying the public eye, as reporters and photographers from a multitude of countries buzzed around. A group of noisy Italian newsmen, making a newsreel for *Giornale Luce*, completed the illusion of a Mediterranean holiday.

To the evident frustration of the Czech welcoming team led by the mayor of Prague, the British ambassador had turned up with two of the leading figures from Henlein's party, both looking supremely confident. I overheard Lady Runciman chatting with them about the "Bolshevik influence in Czechoslovakia". It was swelteringly hot and the British delegation was swept by car the few hundred yards to the Hotel Alcron, just the other side of Wenceslas Square. They lost no time in calling a press conference. The ladies and gentlemen of the press followed on foot, stopping off at the cafés and beer gardens on the way.

The lobby of the Alcron, Prague's most luxurious hotel, was bustling with activity. A hundred and fifty journalists were fighting for space, speaking a dozen different languages; every now and then a tripod or a camera flash crashed to the ground. A wooden dais had been set up in the main lounge.

A fresh-looking Lord Runciman came down from his suite upstairs, but quite suddenly his face fell. There seemed to be a problem, and I was quickly asked to interpret.

Robert Stopford, who seemed by far the most approachable and best-humoured member of the delegation, looked slightly bemused ... "The statue," I overheard Lord Runciman whisper into Stopford's ear. The problem soon became evident. There was a larger than life marble female nude at the back of the lounge, just behind the microphone at which Lord Runciman was to speak. I remembered that the Viscount was a staunch Methodist, teetotal and of strict puritan morality. Stopford went to see if the statue could be moved, but it was very much a fixture. "What a pity she hasn't got wings. She could be represented as an angel of peace," he remarked, well out of earshot of his delegation leader.

I had a word with the eager-to-please hotel manager, and in a few minutes the microphones were moved to another corner. The whole circus with cameras and cables and tripods began again and at last Lord Runciman was able to begin, with proper dignity and aplomb. Aptly enough for a leading British Methodist, he began by quoting John Wesley. "I come as a friend of all and enemy of none ..." And that was pretty much it. At no point in his very carefully worded short speech did he point out that no one in Czechoslovakia, on one side or the other, had actually invited him. Instead he contented himself with the words, "I am delighted that everyone has said that my presence will be welcome." Even that was stretching the truth to its limits.

The delegation scuttled off behind the offending statue as soon as Lord Runciman's comments were over. No questions were taken from the press corps. The more hardened journalists, some of whom were used to reporting from the battlefields of Spain or Abyssinia, were less than impressed by this reticence, as they were politely shaken off with words about a delicate mission and confidentiality-by-necessity.

Formal talks with Beneš, Hodža and Krofta began pretty much straight away, with the delegation, all in top hats and tailcoats despite the heatwave, being whisked off in several gargantuan Hispano-Suiza limousines that blocked the whole street and a good part of Wenceslas Square as well. But what struck me more than this ill-placed British pomp and ceremony was the informality of their talks with Henlein's men. The Sudeten German press spokesman, the omnipresent Herr Ullrich, told me proudly that it had all been carefully prepared – the party had set up a "political staff" to lead the negotiations and a "social staff" to entertain the delegation. It was cynical and brilliant. Henlein knew very well that much of the British establishment already had greater understanding for the Germans than the Czechs. The social staff was headed by Prince Ulrich Kinsky, who organised hunting and fishing parties at his country estates and those of his friends for the aristocratic Runciman, whisking him away every weekend to a different fairy-tale castle.

The delegation had just returned from the latest round of talks with Beneš, which were altogether more formal. Ernst Kundt and Wilhelm Sebekowsky were waiting at the Hotel Alcron at the head of a group of Sudeten German Party politicians, including Gustav Peters whom I remembered well from his display of amateur dramatics in parliament back in March. This was the "political staff" and Ullrich had asked me if I would mind interpreting for them … just informally, you understand. I could not resist the offer.

I did not join them for the initial talks with Runciman, but when the two delegations went to the bar later, minus the teetotal Viscount, I was with them. For the British side it was Stopford and Ashton-Gwatkin who did most of the talking.

It was an odd experience. Kundt, who always managed to sound reasonable and moderate, despite his little Hitler moustache, outlined the differences between his party's stance and that of the Czechoslovak government. "The government thinks only in terms of a Czechoslovak national state." He went on to paint a picture of a second Switzerland, basking in the Central European sun, "What *we* want to create is a state of nationalities." It was all talk of autonomy, respect and recognition. As I translated, I couldn't stop thinking about the gulf between these words and the version of the future I had heard from Kundt's party boss a week earlier amid the crowds in Breslau. He handed out more copies of the Carlsbad demands, and ordered another round of beer.

The party broke into smaller groups, each trying out their language skills – Ashton-Gwatkin remembered his German nanny, who apparently taught the children quite the wrong accent. He tried it out, to much hilarity. A couple of beers later, Kundt cornered Stopford and launched into a monologue which took on a distinctly Teutonic air. Words came thick and fast: *Volksgemeinschaft* and *Führerprinzip*, and then, as he focused on his dreams for the Sudetenland, it was all *Rechtspersönlichkeit* and *Siedlungsgebiet*. Stopford looked to me for help and I was quite literally lost for words. These words could not be translated, and it was not just a question of language. They came from a different planet, but it was a planet that was drawing us into its orbit at great speed.

*

Two weeks went by, Runciman's delegation was completely unwilling to communicate with the press and Bill Morrell was beside himself with anger. "They're like hedgehogs, curling up every time we go near them."

But on one occasion the two of us managed to corner a member of the delegation in the lounge of the Alcron. Avoiding our glance, he stared into his whisky and soda.

"With all due respect, this silence cannot go on indefinitely. Please give us something to go on."

"I'm sorry. I know your difficulty. But these days it's essential that a great deal of our work should remain absolutely confidential. The least leakage may lead to … well, to a war."

"Well, if you consider things as bad as that, don't you think the people in England ought to know something about it?"

"Oh come now."

"But of course, England must never be allowed to think about war until war is about a week away. It's bad for business …" Morrell was fuming but forced himself to remain calm. "Let me put it another way. If we get our news from other sources, will you be in a position to confirm or deny it?"

There was a long pause.

"I don't think I'm entitled to say yes even to that. I can't describe to you fellows how dangerous this situation is."

Our conversation ended abruptly. The delegate jumped up to greet a Sudeten official who had just turned up in a car driven by a young man in party uniform – grey shirt, black trousers, black knee-boots. A few weeks ago Henlein's men would not have dared to show themselves in the centre of Prague in an overtly Nazi uniform. Times were changing. Morrell and I laughed at the idea of party uniforms – I wonder what they'd look like back home. Blue for the Tories, red for Labour. We ordered another whisky.

*

Ilse was not home when I dropped by in Karlín and then I was out when she left a note in Újezd. After another exchange of notes we finally met for a walk with Peter in the park at Letná. Things were getting worse in the Sudetenland and Ilse was concerned about Father Reichenberger. "He has such faith in human nature, but I'm afraid that someone might hurt him or that his nerves might not take it all." In the cool shadow of the chestnut trees we headed slowly towards the edge of the park. Peter was looking forward to a ride on the carousel. The horses looked remarkably lifelike with real horse leather and big glass eyes. "I was scared of them when I was small," Ilse remembered. "In those days the carousel was on the other side of the park. It's nearly fifty years old. Peter loves it." We exchanged stories about our Catholic upbringings with a mixture of nostalgia and exasperation. I had noticed that Ilse and Peter laughed often, and for a while I lost that sense of being in some kind of Wonderland, where certain rules seemed to apply, but I had no idea what they were. "You know," Ilse said, "My father always used to say that we Germans from Bohemia and Moravia are a bit different from the others, that we look on things from outside. That's where our sense of humour comes from." We walked on, with Peter swinging himself round the plane trees lining Kostelní Street. "If we lose our humour, then everything else goes with it."

Difficult Questions

It was the beginning of September and everyone sensed that something was about to happen. The radio headquarters were buzzing with people and languages – literally hundreds of foreign newsmen had turned up.

Runciman's pressure on Beneš was enormous. Everyone could feel it, and the English Lord was becoming the butt of ever more sarcastic Czech jokes. Beneš had offered further sweeping concessions to Henlein – promising everything short of total secession. Morrell and I tried to get close to Beneš's inner circle – to find out what was going on. Shiela Grant Duff invited us to join her in the Press Club near Wenceslas Square, where Czech journalists would often get together. She told me that Hubert Ripka would be there. Ripka was one of the president's closest associates, and an astute political journalist. Clearly the president had failed to consult the latest concessions with him and he was openly angry. Nervous and impatient, he found it hard to contain himself, even in front of foreign journalists. "Czechoslovak public opinion is understandably asking itself and must continue to ask itself whether these concessions are not going too far." The words were dry and diplomatic, but his anger was clear enough. He shook my hand and as he headed for the door, he left us with a message for our countrymen, "I sincerely hope that these sacrifices will be suitably appreciated by the western democracies." Shiela and I said nothing and tried to avoid catching each other's eye.

Over whisky at the Ambassador half an hour later, a British journalist, fresh to this country, asked me if the crisis was over. "Surely Henlein cannot say no to the concessions. He's got all he wants. Total autonomy for the Sudetenland." I expected Shiela to answer, but she looked to me too and I was flattered that she was interested in my point of view. I thought for a minute and began hesitantly. "I'm sure you're right when it comes to most of the Sudeten Germans themselves. They just want to live in peace, but I'm rather afraid that Henlein is heeding the call of a different master." The journalist gave me a knowing nod. As I walked home, I could not help wondering if Henlein didn't feel himself cornered. Everything he had been doing for the last six months had been directed towards securing a complete secession, at the same time sustaining the illusion that he would make do with less. How could he say no to Beneš's latest offer without losing face? For the first time in months, even Henlein's trusty press spokesman Oskar Ullrich was not picking up the telephone.

Henlein himself had gone to Berchtesgaden to consult with the Führer. "Our Führer, who art in Berchtesgaden," Jelínek quipped. My own image of Berchtesgaden was of a fairy-tale castle, submerged in mists and deep forests. Before long I would have the chance to see it for myself.

*

I had underestimated Henlein and his people. If they were cornered, they didn't stay there for long. What happened next was a brilliant piece of Nazi manoeuvring. The following day it became only too clear why we had not been hearing much from the usually ubiquitous Oskar Ullrich, whose buffoonish bluster, shining pate and ridiculous owlish glasses had for a while fooled me into thinking of him as a harmless eccentric. He had an instinctive understanding of the press and was ruthless, hard-working and efficient.

Everyone was waiting for Henlein to respond to the latest concessions, so what was needed was to turn attention back to the Czechs. Ullrich adopted a tried and tested method – a Czech atrocity, proof on the ground that the Czechs could not be trusted to keep their word. It occurred, conveniently, in Ostrava, seven hours away by train. All the foreign correspondents were loitering in the lounges of Prague's hotels, so there were no independent witnesses – just the Czech word against the German word.

It had long been no secret that Germany was smuggling weapons into the border areas in preparation for an uprising. Periodically, arms smugglers had been arrested in Czech police raids. A Sudeten German Party delegation went to visit a group of eighty-two of these smugglers being detained in Ostrava. Using language that they knew western democrats would listen to, they announced that they wanted to make sure the men were being given "decent treatment". A crowd – one of those instant crowds that the Nazis seemed able to whip up in any place at any time – gathered outside the prison and a conveniently spontaneous demonstration began.

But at this stage, I still knew none of this. I was in the lounge of the Hotel Alcron when Henlein's deputy Kundt came running down the stairs past Lord Runciman's naked statue and into the lounge, quivering with rage.

"We've broken off negotiations!"

"But why?"

"A demonstration in Ostrava … charged by Czech mounted police. Dozens of our people have been beaten and one of our deputies horsewhipped. If the Czechs can't even control their local officials … "

I headed straight to the Deutsches Haus to find Ullrich. It was not hard. Rumours of what had happened had already spread, and several journalists were buzzing around him. I politely rejected one of his long Virginia cigars. He launched into an impromptu press statement, adopting his best schoolmaster pose, throwing in a bit of rhyming slang for good measure.

"Now let's get down to the brass tacks." He looked at each of us, to make sure we had understood. "The Czech mounted police lost their nerve, charged at the crowd. The delegation inside the prison heard the screaming and came out. One of the police saw them and forced his horse through the crowd in their direction."

"Didn't the police realise who they were?"

"The deputies were holding up their badges, but the copper struck one of them with his whip regardless. It is as clear as the day is long. Whatever the Czech government promises, it is quite evidently unable to impose its authority on local officials."

"So what now?"

"We broke off negotiations straight away."

At this moment Ullrich stopped dead, his jovial manner gone and his face inscrutable. The little knot of reporters dissolved quickly. As we went down the stairs, he added,

"Join us tomorrow at the Parliamentary Club. The party is giving a press conference."

This was a first. Up to now their meetings with the press had always been informal.

Back at the Alcron, I met a member of the Runciman mission. The Ostrava incident had come at a time so convenient for Henlein that even the mission was sceptical. One of its number, a jovial military man called Sutton-Pratt, was already packing his bags, heading to Ostrava to investigate. I wondered what his investigation would look like, gathering evidence a good two days after the event.

At the press conference, the main speaker was Hans Neuwirth, the party's self-styled legal expert, carrying a suitably bulky bundle of dossiers. I had to nudge Bill Morrell a couple of times to stop him laughing out loud as Neuwirth broke into a squeaky high-pitched imitation of Hitler's theatricals. As he piled on statistics of the wounded prisoners of Ostrava, his voice rose in pitch till he sounded like an angry parrot. Morrell was biting his lip determinedly, from time to time his shoulders would shake. But Neuwirth's little monologue did its job perfectly. Eighty-two prisoners had been fettered and beaten and starved, and to prove that this was not new, he thumped on his dossier with evidence aplenty.

Once again, it was the Czech government that was cornered. The Prime Minister, Milan Hodža announced that the policeman involved had been sacked. Hodža was so determined not to give Henlein an opportunity to end the talks altogether that he suspended the Ostrava police chief too. Morrell tried to phone through to the police station. He was not so interested in the police chief but wanted to know what had become of the constable. With his love of detail, a perfect technique for turning lies into truth, Ullrich had given him the policeman's number – 367. No-one in Ostrava, at the police station or elsewhere, was able to say anything more about his fate, who he was or even whether he actually existed.

We managed to glean a little more later that evening, when Sutton-Pratt returned from his investigation in Ostrava, breathless and slightly euphoric.

"That Sudeten German deputy who claims he was beaten is a thug," he roared with laughter. "He asked for it. He was the one who was beating the policeman. His friends called him Siegfried."

With that he marched off to bed, singing a Wagner aria to himself:

"Schmiede, mein Hammer, ein hartes Schwert."

In Some Quarters

Over breakfast in the Ambassador lounge, Morrell tossed *The Times* to me. It was a day old, dated September 7th. From the way he handled the paper, I concluded it was the bearer of some infectious, fatal disease, and I hesitated before I picked it up.

"Read that paragraph out loud … "

I read slowly, trying to concentrate on what the article was saying. Once or twice I stopped altogether, trying to read between the lines.

> … *if the Sudetens now ask for more than the Czech Government are apparently ready to give in their latest set of proposals, it can only be inferred that the Germans are going beyond the mere removal of disabilities and do not find themselves at ease within the Czechoslovak Republic. In that case it might be worth while for the Czechoslovak Government to consider whether they should exclude altogether the project, which has found favour in some quarters, of making Czechoslovakia a more homogeneous State by the secession of that fringe of alien populations who are contiguous to the nation with which they are united by race.*

In any case the wishes of the population concerned would
seem to be a decisively important element in any solution that
can hope to be regarded as permanent, and the advantages
to Czechoslovakia of becoming a homogeneous State might
conceivably outweigh the obvious disadvantages of losing the
Sudeten German districts of the borderland.

"You know what that means?"

"I'm not sure."

"… in some quarters … "

"It sounds a bit mysterious."

"Quite the contrary. The paper's editor is Geoffrey Dawson."

"Yes."

"He is a close friend of Chamberlain … "

"… er, yes … "

"… and Chamberlain has been working on him for months. He's been trying to do the same thing with my own editor too and he's already got the BBC quite in his pocket. You see, it's all about national interest – when we're on the brink of war, we all have to pull in the same direction … that kind of thing."

"And what about *some quarters*?"

"When *The Times* says that some quarters think Czechoslovakia should give up the Sudetenland, it means that Mr Chamberlain has told the paper to let slip that he has decided once and for all to give the Sudetenland to Hitler. It's as simple as that."

"But he must know that the Czechs will fight."

"Are you quite sure about that? What if the Czechs conclude that Britain might go a step further, and could end up actually siding with the Führer?"

"But that's out of the question."

"Is it? It may look that way to you, but I'm not sure. It isn't that far-fetched. Public opinion is a fickle thing, especially in this day when rumours become truth at the speed of light. And just look at the farmers' party here – for all their patriotic bluster, half of them are already in bed with Henlein. They're terrified of Stalin. Sometimes, if you think you are choosing a lesser of two evils, you forget that both, in the end, are evil. And of course, we can be in no doubt that Henlein's press man Ullrich is following all this closely. Don't forget that he used to live in London in the days when he was peddling Jablonec jewellery instead of world domination. He knows the British press too. Half the papers are owned by Lord Rothermere. And Rothermere was the one who ..."

"... who described what Hitler is doing to the Jews as ... How did he put it...?"

"I think *minor misdeeds* was the term he used."

A Jewish Bolshevik War

"Curiouser and curiouser!" Cried Alice.

In 1914 international Jewry had forced a war on Europe ...
   ... once again it was stirring up nations against one another ...
      ... and the Jewish banks were getting ready for the kill.

"This is Radio *Pravda vítězí*" a pleasant woman's voice announced in Czech. Everywhere there was talk of this new station – *Truth Prevails*. The presenter announced that she was broadcasting from Vienna for the Czech minority in the Ostmark – the Nazis' new name for Austria. Reception was conveniently perfect throughout Czechoslovakia and nobody was in doubt as to who the real intended audience was. The broadcasts were virulently anti-Jewish. It was the kind of language we had heard in German from the Reichssender and seen in some of the leaflets of the Czech fascists, but spoken out on the airwaves in loud, clear and calm Czech, this was new. The words took on flesh and blood.

With strange fascination we all tuned in. There was something hypnotic about this warm, maternal voice with its poisoned message. Miloslav Disman was under no illusions.

He stopped me on the corridor just outside the radio director's office. "I've just been talking to Šourek. I wanted to warn him. People really are beginning to absorb this poison. Can you be surprised when we're telling them next to nothing?"

Apparently Šourek had given no reply.

"People are calling for an iron fist, for a military dictatorship, for the banning of political parties, God knows what else! Remember that tanks and guns are a form of truth too, or at least they create their own truths."

Disman had just returned from visiting relatives in East Bohemia and was still dressed in country clothes, complete with heavy walking boots. He must have been a strange sight in Šourek's immaculate office, with all its chrome and polished wood.

"You have to remember – political battles are nearly always won in the countryside. I've just seen it with my own eyes."

He showed me the traces of the rich red soil of the Giant Mountain foothills still on his boots.

"Farmers mistrust cosmopolitan Prague, and – do you know what? – those Vienna broadcasts aren't as stupid as you think. They never throw their vitriol in the face of the good Czech peasant. Just listen carefully. They rant against all the parties except the Agrarians, all the papers except the farmers' weekly. The Nazis are looking for allies if it comes to invading this country. And it's really not that hard to change people if you say the right things in the right tone."

My memories of Mosley's blackshirt rallies in the East End were still fresh enough. They too had seemed to come from nowhere. And I had no right to claim they had nothing to do with me. Just a few years before, on a bus in Whitechapel, I had become their unwitting accomplice.

*

An outside-broadcast van was being loaded up hurriedly in the drizzle in front of the radio. I was about to cross to the tram stop, but suddenly I heard Disman's voice again. He leapt out of the van and invited me to join him.

"We can just fit you in."

I squeezed into the cab between Disman, who by now had changed into a suit and tie and looked quite the gentleman, and the sound engineer who was driving. With a cheerful apology, the driver put a bulky piece of recording equipment on my lap and we headed down Wenceslas Square to the new traffic lights at Můstek, then through the narrower streets to the Old Town Square. Disman looked up from his notes. "I'm getting quite good at this kind of stuff," he grinned. "Our very own propaganda. Just don't tell Šourek."

The Town Hall had just been renovated. Two eternal flames were blazing from modern steel torches beneath the Gothic oriel of the chapel. It was an impressive sight. Our equipment was set up, drawing much interest from passers-by, and the broadcast began. As I remembered from his recent performance on Wenceslas Square, Disman had a gift for this kind of pathos. "Within," he whispered into the microphone, "the unknown soldier dreams his eternal dream." The Town Hall had been transformed. We went inside and Disman enthused about the new lifts equipped with "the very latest twentieth century technological innovations", sweeping visitors up to the higher floors. The city's mayor, Petr Zenkl appeared beside him and continued in the same spirit:

"This building has been, and will remain, a secure pillar of our freedom."

He was speaking as if its very existence were an inoculation against the forces massing around it, a latter-day equivalent of the Blaník Knights. I'm not sure he would have convinced Bill Morrell.

*

The next day was Saturday 10th September. I joined two young colleagues from Radiojournal for a late lunch in the pub. Both were from abroad, like me, and were working in the English-language shortwave service. They had a thankless job. Day after day, point by point, they would refute the invented claims being fed at frequent intervals through the German radio. Gordon Skilling was a slight, quietly spoken post-graduate history student from Canada. He always had his eyes and ears open to interesting details, and he would note down meticulously what he saw and heard around him. Wilfred Robinson was from Britain. He was a big man, a gentle giant, impulsive and outspoken, determined to do his bit for Czechoslovakia, his adopted home. The two men could not have been more different, and with me, an ungainly teenager alongside them, we must have made a comic threesome.

I spent a lot of time with Robinson during those days. In his three years in Prague he had failed to learn more than the most elementary Czech, but it was a pleasure working with him. *"Dvě piva"* – two beers – was his favourite Czech expression, and it served him well. He was very generous and when we had drunk our beers – usually it was a good deal more than just two – he would always insist on paying. His gentleness was accompanied by a sense of justice, of the same kind I had encountered in Edgar Young.

Gordon walked back to the radio, where he was on weekend duty, while Wilfred and I carried on down Wenceslas Square. In the premature darkness, the persistent drizzle threatened to turn into a downpour, but knots of people were already gathering under the plane trees. President Beneš was about to take to the airwaves. His latest bid for peace, the so-called fourth plan, which had offered the Sudeten Germans nearly everything that Henlein had ever demanded, had led to a deep sense of unease, and his speech was awaited with some apprehension. Beneš was trying to keep war at bay, but it seemed closer than ever. The speech was being broadcast live by Radiojournal and relayed through loudspeakers attached to lampposts on street corners.

Everyday life on the square was going on as usual, with no sign that we were on the edge of the abyss. A little girl, holding her mother's hand, was looking in the window of an antique shop, where colourful folk costumes were on display. Drawn by the sound and smell, the child skipped to the window of Julius Meinl's next door, where an assistant was gathering coffee beans with a big shovel from a huge copper vat. "It's always like that," one of the hardened British war reporters had told me a few days before. He had spent two years in Spain. "One day everything's quite normal – the next day the city's in ruins.

And you can be sure of just one thing … That it will happen when you least expect it."

There were queues building outside some of the shops, people were getting in extra supplies of food. Sometimes you saw someone walking about with a grey cylindrical tin hung around his neck. Gas masks were being issued. There was a gnawing anxiety, but as yet no panic, and I had not heard of any violence against Germans in the city.

"I wonder how much longer this can go on," I turned to Robinson.

"Death is better than slavery," he replied. The ferocity of the gentle giant took me by surprise.

Just before six-thirty, with President Beneš's speech about to begin, the few cars on the square stopped, all the passengers poured out of the trams, and those who could afford it went into the smart cafés on the square to hear the speech in comfort. The rest gathered beneath the loudspeakers. Beneš began to speak.

Drazí spoluobčané …

Dear fellow citizens. I had heard him speak several times earlier in the year, but this time it was different. There was no sign of the slightly smug, even condescending tone that in the past had often marked the way he spoke about the other nations of Czechoslovakia. He summarised his latest offer of autonomy to the Sudeten Germans, and with each point, in his characteristically long, rambling sentences he gave a reassurance that the sovereignty of the country was not under threat. Robinson, who did not speak the language and had nothing but Beneš's voice to go on, suggested that he sounded a little like a father talking to his children as the family set sail on a perilous voyage. He asked me if I thought the speech was aimed at calming fears in Britain and France, but that was not my impression. This was a speech for his own citizens.

I do not speak to the politicians and the political parties. What I have to say is obvious to them. I speak, however, to the individual citizens. I speak to all people. Never in the past has the responsibility of each one of you been greater than it is now.

There was no pretence that the situation was anything other than grave. His voice, monotonous as ever, was painfully sad.

Show the world that no one among us desires to take on himself responsibility for increasing European tension today. Let us not forget that faith and goodwill move mountains.

Beneš was not a natural public speaker, nor was he a great linguist and he sounded awkward as he switched from Czech to Slovak, and then, at the end of the speech, began again in German:

Teuere Mitbürger …

He repeated his message in the same sad tone, matching the rain, which by now had begun to fall steadily, drumming on the umbrellas around us.

Wilfred Robinson and I went out into the middle of the square. Despite the rain, an even larger crowd was gathering, many of them the same people who had been listening to the speech a while before. They were here to witness a strange pageant. A procession was passing through the square; at its head was the Archbishop of Prague, carrying before him the Palladium, a bronze relief of the Virgin and Child that was said to date back to the days of Princess Ludmila in the 10th century.

Tradition had it that the Palladium would protect Bohemia in times of danger. The symbolism was obvious. The celebrations were to mark the 300th anniversary of the Palladium's return, after being carried off to Germany as booty during the Thirty Years War. I felt that I had drifted into a historical novel. It became even more unreal when we reached the top of the square. I spotted none other than Miloslav Disman beneath the statue of Saint Wenceslas, commenting on everything around him into the microphone. *"And now, a few lines from our poet, František Halas ... "* And he began to recite from memory:

> *Do not forget the chorale*
> *O you of little faith*
> *Do not forget the chorale.*

Disman went on solemnly, reaching new levels of pathos ...

> *The Palladium, sanctified with tears of suffering and with entreaties for peace and goodwill among men and peoples, is making its pilgrimage through the streets of Prague like the eloquent voice of the Christian tradition of Cyril and Methodius and Saint Wenceslas and as evidence of the centuries-old existence of a state that was not founded just twenty years ago, but rather renewed.*

To the accompaniment of the Saint Wenceslas Chorale sung by a male voice choir, and headed by veterans of the Great War, the procession inched its way up to the National Museum and beyond. The stone cobbles glistened in the rain and I felt chilled to the bone.

I heard my name called. It was a familiar voice. The Sudeten German "Red Chaplain" from Liberec, Father Reichenberger, was sheltering from the rain by the steps of the museum. He stepped out and greeted me, as always, like an old friend.

"Surprised to see an old Teuton like me?" he asked. He drew me closer. "Don't forget your history. The Palladium of the Blessed Virgin and Child is a symbol of the protection of the Lands of Bohemia against Protestantism!" He gave a sad little laugh. "It's nothing to do with nationality or language." A short history lesson followed. "Remember, the Palladium only survived the Thirty Years War by being smuggled to the safety of Vienna when the Swedes marched into Stará Boleslav. I don't think those Nordic hordes would have had much time for our Blessed Virgin." He had the gentle smile of a priest accustomed to offering solace to members of his flock, but his eyes showed nothing but sorrow, as he went on. "It breaks my heart. All the time, as I followed the procession, I never dared to open my mouth. As a German I would not have been welcome. Even within the church we are all marked now by the language we speak."

I did not know what to say in reply. Throughout my childhood priests had been figures of authority and certainty, but now Father Reichenberger seemed utterly alone. I could think of nothing better than to stammer an invitation to join me in the warmth of one of the cafés, which had stayed open late for the crowds, but he declined politely, shook my hand and walked away. I watched the lonely figure, as he carried on in the direction of Saint Ludmila, remote from the teeming mass around him. I shivered. Crowds of Czech patriots were passing, somewhere among them the enthusiastic Wilfred Robinson. It was still raining, but I had no desire to go home. I found shelter in the Hotel Ambassador, where I ordered a whisky and sat alone in the corner of the lobby.

At midnight Bill Morrell walked in. His fox terrier barked a couple of times and wagged his tail cheerfully when he saw me. We sat until the early hours in the half-darkness of the bar where many of the lights had been dimmed in anticipation of the blackout that would inevitably come in the event of mobilisation. Morrell, never at home in the suspended reality of city hotels and sensing that something was about to explode, asked me if I would like to take another trip with him to the Sudetenland. "It will cheer you up," he joked. "We leave first thing Monday morning."

Visions

The weather in Prague was as bad as ever, but by the time we reached the edge of the city, the sun had come out, giving us a clear view of the distant peaks of the Středohoří – the Mittel-gebirge – the volcanic hills north of Prague that had so inspired the romantics of the nineteenth century, both Czech and German. By now the hops had been gathered, and elsewhere the ploughed fields were a rich red. There were ripe apples and plums on the trees that lined the road, and occasionally we would pass a woman in a headscarf gathering the fruit in a wicker basket or a wooden barrow.

It was not hard to find a hotel in Carlsbad. Few people were taking the waters, and the colonnades were occupied by a hand-ful of elderly men, playing chess. The current drama had emp-tied the spas and hotels even more than the economic crisis that had crippled the economy of the Sudetenland.

As the sun broke again through the clouds and we walked down towards the Sudeten German Party headquarters, our spirits rose a little and we stopped for a glass of wine on the empty terrace of the Goldenes Schild. The waiter was Czech and nervously mixed Czech, German and broken English as he took our order. The radio inside was tuned to the Reichssender Breslau, playing a lively dance tune. It was a familiar American number, but the lyrics were German. *Sie will nicht Blumen und nicht Schokolade, sie will immer, immer wieder mich ...* For about a year now, it had been forbidden to play songs with English lyrics in the Reich, but the German affection for swing was stubbornly resilient.

From the terrace we watched as loudspeakers were set up at the corner of one of the houses opposite, just as they had been on Wenceslas Square two days before. A group of boys, all around sixteen or seventeen, marched past the hotel, several of them carrying what I later realised were huge rolled swastikas. Had I been less dulled by the wine and the spa town sense of timelessness, perhaps I would have sensed what was in the air.

Everyone was waiting for the live broadcast of Hitler's speech, the culmination of the six-day Nazi Party rally in Nuremberg. "The Führer is going to talk about us," one uniformed lad told us proudly when he noticed we were foreigners.

At around six we arrived at the Sudeten German Party head-quarters just around the corner from the colonnade. There were a few party officials running in all directions, clearly very busy, and we were shown up to the party treasurer's apartment two floors above.

A woman in her fifties opened the door, greeting us with *"Heil Hitler!"* as she untied her apron, folded it carefully and led us into the sitting room. "Come in! He is due to speak any minute." Morrell nudged me with his elbow and gestured towards a pho-tograph of Henlein on the mantelpiece. He was posing, stand-ing very straight and looking sternly into the distance. Ranged round the photograph were three boys – her sons, she told us, as she noticed the direction of our glance. in a few minutes one of them came in, a bright, alert lad, about sixteen years old, who clicked his heels and said *"Heil Hitler!"* in greeting.

Chairs were brought in and we all sat round the radio. After a couple of minutes the music stopped and a harsh voice cried *"Der Führer hat das Wort."*

Morrell took out his notebook, watched by the boy, who was sitting as close to the radio as he could. Hitler began on familiar territory, attacking democracy and the Jews. Morrell whispered in my ear, "Amazing, isn't it? That he should open the most important speech of his life with these two threadbare subjects." Our hosts gave us a stern glare, and we sat in silence as the Führer sneered at the world's democracies. It was nothing new ... the only two nations in Europe supported by 99 per-cent of their peoples were Germany and Italy ... that was true democracy. He poured contempt on England for its hypocrisy in condemning the bombing of the Abyssinians while bomb-ing the Arabs of Palestine into submission. The boy and his mother watched us curiously. "I suppose they expected us to blush," Morrell remarked later.

The next part of the speech seemed quite incongruous amid all the trappings and comfortable *Gemütlichkeit* of this middle-class spa-town apartment. Hitler painted a picture of tortured Sudeten Germans. The way he articulated the word *gequält* evoked images of the most gruesome suffering. The Sudeten Germans were being subject to a slow process of extermination, *Vernichtung*. They were not even allowed to sing the songs they loved. Here he was referring to the Nazi marching songs that had become so popular in the Sudeten German sports clubs.

The lad's lip was trembling with emotion. With his reason, he would have known that this was all vast exaggeration, but the Führer was not calling to his reason.

The speech shifted to another favourite subject – German re-armament. As Hitler recited the numbers of men and of tons of material which his fortifications had taken up, the boy's mother seemed to become a little restless. She went back out into her kitchen and we could hear the sound of pots and pans being tidied up. Morrell nudged me again, and we both looked towards the boy. He didn't even seem to know we were there, his head pillowed on his arms, huddled up to the loud-speaker, listening avidly, his bright eyes darting around the room, seeing visions …

The Führer had given assurances that Germany would not leave her fellow Germans to be suppressed and humiliated – *weder wehrlos noch verlassen.*

The lad immediately leapt up, put on his boots and hurried out, without even a glance in our direction. By the time his mother came back from the kitchen, doing her best not to look concerned, he was long gone. We took our leave, and she, politely and a little nervously, acknowledged our thanks with a nod. We went out into the street. At first all was quiet. Then from somewhere we heard the banned *Horst Wessel Song.* People poured out of cafés and pubs and joined the procession, men and women, six in a row, marching in military tempo. *Die Fahne hoch! Die Reihen fest geschlossen!*

In a couple of minutes we reached a square of open ground, surrounded by market stalls, which we could just make out in the half dark. People were stretching into the distance. Flags were waving, the forbidden swastika flags. I looked out for the uniformed lad we had seen earlier and for the boy from the flat we had just left, but they had disappeared in the mass. The crowd was surging, their cries heaving with the movement. Somebody was arranging a spotlight on the second-storey balcony of a house. A group of figures appeared at the window and came onto the balcony. The cheering strengthened. One of the figures raised his hands. The spotlight lit his face. I saw he was speaking but his sentences were snatched away by the cheers. Phrases reached me, and between us Morrell and I were able to put a few fragments together: "Have patience … we will soon be free … the Leader has spoken …" Flags were waved above the sea of upturned faces.

We had seen enough and started back through the town to the Goldenes Schild. It was quieter here, although the roar of the crowd was loud enough to reach every corner of the town and echo from the forests on the valley sides. In a side street we heard the crash of glass. They were smashing shop windows. Soon the sound was answered by more glass breaking, this time from another direction. There were no police about. Cautiously, we followed the sound. In the window of a clothes shop, a group of young men was kicking at a number of figures who lay motionless on the ground, their arms and legs twisted. One of the legs flew out onto the pavement. The figures were mannequins. The crowd laughed. Another young man appeared carrying a tin and a brush. He painted a large, dripping Star of David on the front door. The white paint seemed to glow in the darkness.

Without being noticed, we turned back. Morrell whispered to me. "Where are the other newsmen? Are we to be the only independent witnesses of all this?" He quickened his pace, struggling to control his anger. His question didn't need an answer. All the correspondents would be in the bar of the Ambassador in Prague, watching history through the bottom of a whisky glass. I would have been there too, if he had not invited me to join him.

By midnight the crowds had begun to disperse, but there was hardly a Czech or Jewish owned shop that had not been in some way damaged; Czech gendarmes and soldiers were beginning to venture cautiously into the streets. I could see the headlines in the German papers tomorrow – martial law, police brutality. Nothing about what had actually been happening – and the reality was that something very dark indeed had occurred in Carlsbad that night, and, as I found out later, in dozens of other towns in the Sudetenland.

We knew that the rules of the game had changed. From now on, it was all or nothing – there would be no more pretending that the Sudeten German Party wanted nothing more than autonomy. The choice was stark: either the Czechs concede or there will be war.

Radio had played an awful role at that moment. Like an angry god, Hitler had used radio to cast rods of hatred through the ether, yet the eyes of the world had remained turned to the hypnotizing spectacle of Nuremberg itself rather than the places to which Hitler's words were directed. In the Sudetenland itself, it was crystal clear that Hitler had drawn the battle lines that night.

*

We were not surprised the next day to find the Sudeten German Party headquarters in Carlsbad empty, including the shelves and the safe – and it was not the Czech gendarmes who had carried the material away. Henlein and his men had crossed to the Reich to prepare the revolution. I went upstairs, past the door of the now firmly locked party treasurer's office to the flat where we had listened to the speech the previous evening. The woman did not seem pleased to see me – there was no sign of any of her three sons; her eyes were red, and I noticed that the radio was covered with a cloth that for a moment reminded me of a shroud. Evidently, she had no plans for further listening. As I walked slowly back down the stairs I understood what had happened. Her sons, including the sixteen-year-old we had met yesterday, had left for the Reich to get ready to fight. I was sure that she had little doubt what that meant. I wondered how many brothers and cousins she had lost in the Great War.

Simultaneity

Nuremberg, August 1950

In a bare room, in an ugly new hotel on the edge of a city still in ruins, I took a slim folder out of my briefcase. It held a few letters and cuttings that I had kept since 1938. With them, I pieced together the scenes that I had heard but not seen that September night. Radio, with its power to conjure up the darkest spirits of the night and diffuse them at the speed of light, had infected my mind that evening, and through the years that followed, those spirits had continued to haunt me.

Nuremberg itself released few clues of its dark recent past. The huge Parteigelände was a kitchen garden, feeding a city overcrowded with refugees, Germans from the east, a good number of them from the Sudetenland. Part of the area was being used by the Americans to store munitions. The shell-pocked buildings were crumbling and weeds were breaking through the granite of the parade road, as if it had been abandoned by Roman legions in times long past. Elsewhere, sticks of peas and beans were marching across the grounds.

It was no longer easy to imagine the moment when Hitler had greeted nearly a quarter of a million brown-shirted supporters on the Zeppelinfeld and then taken to the airwaves. I took an envelope out of the folder, already yellowing and brittle. It was a letter my mother had sent to me, postmarked September 14th 1938, which she must have written just hours after the events I had witnessed in Carlsbad. Inside there were several newspaper cuttings. During my stay in Prague she would quite often send bits and pieces that she thought would interest me, and one of the cuttings with the letter was from *The Times* at the height of the party rally. It described the spectacular light show that Albert Speer had conjured up for the Führer, with beams of light shining twenty-five thousand feet into the night sky. According to the article, the British Ambassador, Nevile Henderson, had been little short of ecstatic. He compared it to being inside a cathedral of ice.

Sitting at the spindly pine table in my hotel room, I reread my mother's letter. For a moment I hesitated. I had not seen her handwriting for several years: deliberate, neat and un-English. She had died not long after the war, suddenly, from pneumonia, and in the months beforehand I had seen her only once. Anna had hinted at reproach when she died, but nothing was said openly. Now, with the letter as a scrap of evidence before me, I imagined Máma – we always called her in the Czech way, with a stress on the long first "a" – at the little desk by the window in our front room, writing carefully and conscientiously to a son in the eye of the storm. I read the last page, which happened to be the first that I pulled from the envelope.

... The atmosphere is nervous here in London; air raid shelters are being built, we are being issued gas masks. I shall be fetching mine tomorrow. As you know, there is talk of mobilisation. I listened to Hitler's speech on the wireless last night. We all did. The BBC interrupted the evening programme again and again to bring reports from Nuremberg. It was all so venomous. It's so hard for us to grasp what is happening, but that man's tone seems clear enough. I almost envy the English, not being able to understand him. Some are saying that this means war. Others are relieved that Hitler didn't actually declare war there and then.

The letter surprised me with its meticulous documentary detail, and with hindsight I realised that this was her way of keeping her fears at bay or at least making sure that I was not troubled by them. It went through my mind that she would have been a good journalist, as her thoughts were always ordered, far more so than my own. I read on.

This morning's papers have dubbed last night "Hitler Night". Apparently, thousands of people gathered outside Downing Street and booed at the theatre-goers in their evening finery – saying they shouldn't have been out on the town on such a night. In New York they even closed Wall Street. I really don't know what to expect. Anna and I both embrace you and wish you a safe homecoming. You are in our thoughts always.

Líbám Tě
Máma

As I had sat with Morrell listening on the radio to Hitler's speech in that neat flat in Carlsbad, the eardrums of my mother and my sister and so many millions of others across the world had been beating to the same rhythm. This was a very new kind of simultaneity.

The Ten Commandments

On the morning of September 14th I received an urgent phone call from Morrell. Hitler and Chamberlain were going to meet in Bavaria. His editor wanted him to cover the meeting, but he would rather continue monitoring what was going on in the Sudetenland – the litmus for truth and lies, as he put it. So he asked me to go to Bavaria. Thanks to radio, with its appetite for instant news day and night, both journalism and diplomacy had begun to move at a breathtaking pace. Claims were asserted and denied within minutes, demands were made, rejected, amended and rejected again, all in the space of a few hours, and we, the public, were glued to our radio sets, following each step as it happened, trying to make sense of claim and counterclaim, guessing at what might be truth, exaggeration or downright lie. Truth will prevail, but just make sure it is *my* truth that prevails.

I was nervous and protested to Morrell that I was not a journalist, but he would have none of it. "You're perceptive. Just write what you see. I've already sorted out accreditation and my editor has no problem with it." Somewhat dazed, a couple of hours later I was heading not for Munich, but Berlin, as the Germans had arranged a special train to take journalists from the capital all the way to Berchtesgaden, where the meeting was to take place. The weather was extremely cold for mid-September and immediately I regretted not packing warmer clothes.

There were chaotic scenes at Berlin's Friedrichstrasse station. I caught a glimpse of the headline in the evening paper, the *Nachtausgabe*, in bold type: "Czech Troops Have Launched an Attack on the German Empire". Nearly a hundred international journalists had turned up, and while we waited for the train to arrive, the indefatigable Bill Shirer from CBS set up a portable transmitter, about the size of a suitcase, on the platform. He was sending live impressions to New York, describing the bustle around him and I had the feeling that for many listeners in America this was their first insight into how much radio had transformed the work of the journalist.

"Looking at the lines under my colleagues' eyes, I can see they haven't had much sleep, working fifteen to twenty hours a day. Right now, for example."

The station was full of noise. The electric suburban trains of the Stadtbahn were passing in all directions, packed with people heading home from work.

The suitcases of the press folk were lying as if randomly scattered across the platform, but it soon became clear that everything was quite under control. The German government's press representative, Dr Bremer, had an eye for detail and he watched over us like an English butler. No one was to miss the train. Bill Shirer's microphone was still open and he was catching the passing correspondents for a word or two. The only woman in the group, Sigrid Schulz from the *Chicago Tribune*, was talking. "As long as the talks go on, war won't break out." Next to her stood Pete Huss from the International News Service, looking dishevelled, out of breath and deathly pale. He tried to conjure up something of the life of the newsman in the last few weeks. He hadn't slept for two days … in his rush to get to the station he had even forgotten his typewriter … even so he knew that whatever he did, Hitler would keep a step ahead and he would get "nothing but a horse laugh and a squawk from the boss in New York."

I admired and envied these American correspondents. They were enjoying the adventure of it all, they were untiring, unflappable, and their editors in New York or Chicago not only welcomed their risks and experiments – like the crazy idea of broadcasting live from a railway station on the way to a press conference – but actually expected it from them.

"Five more minutes," Dr Bremer announced as if dinner were about to be served. I heard the rain beginning to patter on the roof of the station high above us. "Just like back home," I said to Selkirk Panton from the *Express*. He had a heavy cold and muttered his conspiracy theory that Hitler had thought up this whole crisis just as a way of punishing the foreign newsmen for what the world press was writing about the new Germany.

The train drew in and the eighty-one men and one woman of the press stepped onto three special Pullman coaches. We were off to the mountains to see the Führer.

*

The weather in the Bavarian Alps was even worse than in Berlin, and the mist so thick that we might just as well have been on the plains of East Prussia. The post-office in Berchtesgaden was overwhelmed as we fought to get a line out to our editors and I was beginning to regret having come at all. We caught a brief glimpse of Chamberlain, whose ever-present umbrella for once looked set to serve him well as heavy clouds rolled down the mountain. I remembered how I had once walked with my mother through the City of London on a summer afternoon when I was four or five. We had counted the umbrellas and I had imitated the stiff gait of the city gents.

A German government Mercedes swept Chamberlain up to Hitler's nest above the town. He disappeared into the fog like Moses on Mount Sinai.

We waited in the packed cafés of the little Bavarian resort, the geraniums and the tightly laced dirndls of the waitresses oddly incongruous with what we were hearing on the radio. The German wireless was full of talk of a new Czech massacre in the Sudetenland – three hundred unarmed Sudeten civilians murdered. The message was clear. The Sudeten crisis must be resolved immediately. Otherwise we shall face a humanitarian crisis on a huge scale. Germany cannot sit and wait while Germans are being murdered in cold blood.

Of one thing I was sure: that the massacre was the first thing Hitler brought up when he spoke to Chamberlain, and I rather doubted that Chamberlain had any way of checking the story, up there in the misty heights of Hitler's mountain retreat.

It seemed that he was not that bothered anyway. When he returned several hours later, flanked by Ribbentrop on one side and his umbrella on the other, the Prime Minister was radiant. It was clear that the visit had gone well. The Führer had put forward conditions for the annexation of the Sudetenland

and Chamberlain had made it clear that he felt them to be reasonable enough. The peace of Europe was in Prague's hands. Meanwhile Ribbentrop's expression betrayed nothing.

As we left the little Alpine town for Oberwiesenfeld airport, amid dozens of girls in plaits and lads in lederhosen, I managed to exchange a few words with Sir Horace Wilson, Chamberlain's senior advisor. He said he had just been in touch with the British mission in Prague. There was no truth at all behind the German wireless rumours. No massacre, nor even a hint of a massacre, had occurred. Nothing. But that, of course, was not the point.

A very young German reporter standing next to me informed me with evident pride that Chamberlain and Ribbentrop were being driven to the airport by the Führer's personal chauffeur. We followed at some distance, in one of several cars that had been laid on for the press. As we approached the airfield we drove through further jubilant crowds. The Reichssender was commenting on the whole event live, as we could hear through loudspeakers around the airfield.

The weather has turned marvellous, a gentle breeze, swastikas and flags of Great Britain are waving high on their masts above us and the British prime minister will have a good flight home.

As the sun broke through the clouds, Mr. Chamberlain had a few concise words for the press and the crowds. He was clearly in good spirits as he thanked all around him for their warm and friendly reception. Then, raising his hat, he bid von Ribbentrop a cheerful *"Au revoir."* I noticed that von Ribbentrop returned a frosty little laugh, also caught on the microphone, a little scrap of evidence for the future.

I sat in a pub near the airfield and took out my notebook to write up Chamberlain's visit for Morrell's paper. Looking out, I saw occasional knots of people, walking home in high spirits. I was exhausted and found it difficult to maintain any distance from all that had been happening in the last few days. I could speak three languages, yet I could not find the words. I was registering everything like a camera, but nothing was in focus. The meanings of the words were swimming. In the article, I stated the barest facts, but even they did not come easily.

Alice laughed: "There's no use trying," she said; "one can't believe impossible things."

"I daresay you haven't had much practice," said the Queen. "When I was younger, I always did it for half an hour a day. Why, sometimes I've believed as many as six impossible things before breakfast."

*

Paní Lašková was walking with her slop bucket across the courtyard, putting it down at each slow step. "What's the time, young man? Morning or evening?" Distracted and for once failing to answer, I hurried to the broadcasting house to meet Wilfred Robinson. He was far from being the only foreign journalist in the building. The Americans had been sending report after report, using shortwave feeds, and, as part of a deal with the radio director Šourek, the US networks had even begun relaying Radiojournal's own shortwave broadcasts to listeners back home. The atmosphere was refreshing – international and open-minded – a reminder of everything that was so quickly being sucked out of Czechoslovakia.

Correspondents had come from across the world, but there was no one from the BBC.

Disman laughed. "Mr Shirer will be able to tell you more about that …"

Bill Shirer from CBS had just arrived from Berlin, looking shabby in his raincoat for all seasons. He recognised me immediately. Chomping cheerfully on a doughnut, he asked if I'd recovered from the *Dunst und Nebel* of the Berchtesgaden escapade.

"Our European office is in the BBC headquarters in London," he explained, "So we're their guests. Not welcome guests, I should add, and we're paying a good few dollars for the privilege of being there. And I have a suspicion that the BBC chiefs trust us just about as much as Herr Hitler."

I must have looked surprised. Shirer went on, "You know what they're calling the disgruntled BBC reporters who have dared to question Chamberlain's policies? The Warmongers. And they are being thoroughly censored. Every word that goes on air is monitored by the Foreign Office. They're not even letting the BBC send correspondents out into the field. Apparently it's un-British!"

"You see how lucky we are?" Disman replied. "Our bosses haven't yet noticed that we're doing most of our work behind their backs."

*

Bill Morrell had just returned from Liberec and he reported that the atmosphere had relaxed enormously in the few days since Henlein and his henchmen had fled to the Reich. People were even joking in the streets about Henlein's unseemly disappearance. *"Der Führer ist geflohen. Kämpfen soll das Volk!"* – The leader has fled. Let the people fight – one stallholder selling Leitmeritz apples on the square had commented sarcastically and, Bill told us, the others around him were just as contemptuous.

Sudeten democrats were also making themselves heard. A group, including Father Reichenberger and Wenzel Jaksch set up what they called the National Council of Peace-Loving Sudeten Germans. Too little, too late, was the usual comment in Prague, but this was a crack in the Nazi armour, a reminder that the Sudetenland was not yet enclosed in the fortress of the Reich. Disman invited Reichenberger and Jaksch, to give talks on Radiojournal. He made sure that their words were broadcast not just in German through the new Prag II transmitter, but also in Czech, and then for the shortwave service abroad in English and French translations. The foreign reporters, by now a permanent feature in the radio building, listened in silence to Father Reichenberger's sombre sermon.

The Father looked pale and grim as he walked up to the microphone. He coughed. The red light on the desk in front of him came on.

> *I speak as a German who truly loves his people and home, and wishes to protect them from destruction. We must not bear the burden of the hatred and curses of the rest of the world.*

His talk was a direct appeal to his fellow Sudeten Germans to turn against Hitler and Henlein. He spoke with the same simple clarity and moral authority as when he had read from the Gospel to his congregation in Wiese; his voice was firm, but slow and sad, as if he were ploughing through heavy clayey mud.

> *I speak as a human being and a Christian, who sees God's image in every human soul, who believes in worthier ways of settling human and inter-state differences than war and annihilation after two thousand years of Christian experience. I speak as a priest who feels unable to bless weapons which ultimately destroy everyone and everything.*

As he paused I was reminded of the moment when he had raised his head to look over his uneasy congregation in Wiese, as if to check that the message had reached them.

> *The agitation must end. It not only endangers life and limb, it is a blow against peace. At such a time it is veritable high treason against our own people. The anonymous agitators have sought safety across the border, but it will be you who must bear the consequences of the incitement – you, Sudeten German men and women and your children. Everyone must be an apostle of peace, in the home circle, at work, in your daily relationships. Sudeten German men and women, think of your responsibility to your family before God, your home and our people. Pray, work, sacrifice for peace. God wishes it.*

The studio engineer recorded Father Reichenberger's words for rebroadcast to different time zones later. At the same time they were imprinted on my memory.

"He has said it all," one of the more hardened American war correspondents whispered, "and I never thought I'd say that of a man of the cloth."

The priest exchanged places at the microphone with his old friend Wenzel Jaksch. They shook hands in silence. Jaksch spoke in the soft German of the South Bohemian countryside, but his words were tough. He was outspoken, not sparing the Czechoslovak government itself.

> We do not want to hear any more promises. We want a
> national peace treaty on the basis of full equal rights, which
> must not be just a scrap of paper, but must be guaranteed in
> every direction. But above all we want peace. We cannot be
> forever objects of power politics. We want to assume our daily
> work again. Let us join all our forces to avoid that our home
> borderland will become a cause of conflict or a battlefield.
> Let us create a higher standard of cooperation of the two
> nationalities who dwell upon a soil assigned to them by destiny
> and which are called to be the bridge linking the German and
> Slav peoples.

As Jaksch finished, I caught Ivan Jelínek's eye. He repeated the gesture I remembered from my very first visit to the radio, feeling around him with his eyes shut like blind justice.

*

A huge demonstration of Henlein's people was called in Dresden, close enough to Czechoslovakia to make the message clear, but safely within the Reich. For days, Henlein's militia, the *Freikorps*, had been making incursions across the border, and through the radio Henlein had been calling on German, Hungarian and Slovak conscripts in the Czechoslovak army to desert. The parade was to show the physical force behind the words. It went without saying that the speeches were being relayed by the Reichssender.

In Prague it was the first really warm afternoon for ages, so I opened the door and sat outside to listen, at the top of the winding steps that led down to the little courtyard. The broadcast had already begun. I recognised the voice. It was Wilhelm Sebekowsky, a Sudeten German politician I had met on several occasions. He had always had the manner of a bright, well-spoken young lawyer, elegant and charming, dressed in a dapper, well-pressed suit. Yet now his voice was a flood of noise, seeping into every synapse of my brain, as I sat staring blankly at the flaking plaster of the old wall opposite. Each sentence ended with a wild and prolonged roar.

Hearing an excited, belligerent crowd on the radio is even more frightening than seeing it on newsreel. There it has a face, or a thousand faces, and somewhere in the background you can nearly always pick out a few people, beyond the edge of the crowd, who are carrying on with their daily lives; at the very least you can imagine a world beyond the mass. But this assault left no such gaps.

We shall be back … but with weapons in our hands...

Battle on the Airwaves

Rumours were spreading that the Czech government and Beneš himself were on the brink of agreeing to give up the borderlands. The pressure was enormous. The British Ambassador Basil Newton and his French counterpart de Lacroix were reported to be travelling back and forwards to Prague Castle day and night, tightening the screw. At the British Embassy, no one was answering the telephone.

Nervous crowds were building up again beneath the loudspeakers on Wenceslas Square. An announcement was about to be made. There were policemen everywhere, but they were making no attempt to restrain the crowd, some were even engaging in conversation with little groups of people, all in animated discussion. With me were Joan and Jonathan Griffin, an English couple who had arrived here at the beginning of the month. They were working on a book about the crisis. Their slightly stiff aristocratic bearing – both were immaculately turned out – made them seem out of place. Was it my imagination or were they thinner and half a head taller than everyone else around? We soon started talking about Chamberlain and the pressure he was putting on Czechoslovakia. They both spoke with outrage; they felt their prime minister's behaviour as a personal affront. On first impression, Joan seemed the tougher of the two and she was almost shaking with anger. She had a Czech tricolour pinned to her collar.

Everyone knew what was coming. On the stroke of 8 p.m. the news was confirmed – this time not by President Beneš or his prime minister, but from the lips of none other than the hugely popular Shakespearean actor, Zdeněk Štěpánek. For a second, truth and fiction mixed. Štěpánek had played the General in *White Disease*, and it was in that role that I imagined him as he spoke. What was he doing here? His voice was deep and full of pathos, he appealed to people to have understanding for their government. A great sacrifice had been made for peace in Europe. The borderlands were to be ceded to Germany.

The whole scene struck an oddly artificial note. I had the feeling that the people around me had no intention of accepting the role that was being asked of them and allowing themselves to become passive victims of the malign gods in a Greek tragedy. "The General has spoken!" someone shouted out, others laughed sarcastically.

The atmosphere was electric and for a moment I wondered whether the crowd would storm the parliament or the Deutsches Haus, home of the now abandoned headquarters of the Sudeten German Party. Or perhaps they would all head towards the Castle or the German, British or French Embassies? But almost immediately – and as I later realised, quite consistently with the logic of the moment – the crowd surged in the opposite direction, up the hill towards Fochova Street. The news had come through the airwaves, and it was through the airwaves that it could be reversed.

Breaking into the broadcasting house was not hard. Nobody was interested in stopping them. Somewhere I heard glass breaking and for a second I was taken back to Carlsbad. It was one of the entrance doors, cracking under the pressure of the crowds. But there was no other sign of violence, just plenty of words. Someone was earnestly trying to explain to a police officer that the only thing the crowd wanted was to be offered a microphone, to tell the world that the country was ready to fight to keep its independence.

Two or three senior radio staff were running frantically back and forth on the stairs, yelling, calling for police reinforcements. At one point one of them took a fire hose, which he threatened to turn on the crowds. I was beginning to be afraid when out of nowhere the chief conductor of the radio orchestra Otakar Jeremiáš appeared, his baton still in his hand. He roared something to his colleague with the hose who withdrew instantly. Then, remaining quite calm, he took the man who had been asking for a microphone by the arm and offered to take him to the broadcasting studio. The atmosphere calmed immediately. I followed them up the stairs. The man, still out of breath, sat down and began to speak: to address the nation.

Radio, in that moment, was more important than parliament or Prague Castle itself. The man's words were confused. He stumbled, contradicted himself, sometimes stopped altogether or repeated whole sentences, all in a grating, cracked voice. He had been cast into history by chance, but he captured a mood. *Let us defend our country*. I do not know how many people across Czechoslovakia heard his words.

The demonstrations continued into the night and through the next morning when a huge crowd gathered on the square in front of the parliament, and then the prime minister resigned. Beneš appointed General Syrový, the one-eyed hero of the Battle of Zborov in the Great War, to replace him, and the news was received with an excitement little short of euphoric.

It looked but did not feel like a military coup. Joan Griffin was vehement. "This is not a government of generals," she insisted, when we met at the radio the following evening. Most of the mess had been tidied up, but there were a couple of extra policemen outside. "This is a democratic state getting ready to defend itself against dictatorship."

I wondered if others in the British press – those who were not actually here – would see it her way.

There is one image from those hours that I will never forget: Otakar Jeremiáš, standing at the top of the stairs with his baton, for a moment looking for all the world as if he were conducting the whole surreal drama.

Last Territorial Demand

In the meantime, events had been moving apace in Germany. Neville Chamberlain had travelled to Bad Godesberg to meet the Führer, his second flight to Germany in a week. Ignoring totally all that had been happening in Prague, Chamberlain had high hopes that Beneš's acceptance of the Berchtesgaden conditions would result in a peaceful settlement with Hitler, and make it possible to carve up Czechoslovakia without further ado. I tuned into the BBC as it went live to Heston Aerodrome for the British Prime Minister's return. I was expecting him to sound triumphant, but the mood was very different. Clearly something in Godesberg had not gone well. Even the door of the plane refused to open. Various background noises could be heard through the air and I sensed the accidental comedy of the scene. "Perhaps," the BBC announcer commented with unintended irony, "someone at the other end was making quite sure that it was shut tightly." When Chamberlain was eventually liberated he was uncharacteristically short of words.

We were soon to find out what had happened in Germany. Hitler had made further demands, including a request for approval of an immediate military occupation of the Sudetenland.

Adding a final touch to Prague's diplomatic isolation in the region, he had also piled on the territorial claims of Hungary and Poland who wanted their own chunks of the rump Czechoslovakia. He had changed the game yet again and Chamberlain was left to feel a fool. Later the BBC announced drily that the British government no longer felt itself to be in a position to call on Czechoslovakia not to mobilise her armed forces. Next morning, for the second time in ten days, I woke up in a Prague preparing for war.

Trenches were being dug, gasmasks issued, windows boarded against air raids. Passing Klárov in the tram, I saw that half the park had been dug up for a shelter. The American reporters were frantically filing dispatches home.

In the Hotel Ambassador that evening I sat for a while in the bar with Eleanor Whitmore. She was enjoying a whisky, having just walked down from the radio to send one of her regular live updates to New York. On the East Coast it was six hours earlier than in Prague and she had a long night ahead of her. Her boss wanted a final roundup at midnight New York time.

"Have you seen what it looks like out there, or rather what it doesn't look like? I was nearly run over by a car, it had no lights at all. I thought I had just fallen into a pot of ink." Eleanor was right. The whole city was pitch black. "Normally Wenceslas Square wouldn't be far off Broadway in the brilliancy of its electric signs at night. Now look at it. I could scarcely make out the sidewalk. The street was like a charcoal line drawn through a pool of tar." She lit another cigarette and emptied her glass. "These are tarry times. Dark, dirty and malodorous."

We talked for a while about what the mobilisation might mean, but I was tired and made my excuses to leave. "Don't get me wrong," Eleanor called as I headed for the revolving door and the gloom outside, "I don't think war is about to break out. Not yet. Hitler's nearly got what he wants already. He'll play with the mouse a bit before killing it." I walked home in the darkness. It was true. Prague was preparing for war, yet it looked uncannily like a city that had fallen into a hundred-year sleep.

The next morning, German radio, with simple logic, declared that Beneš was behind the latest escalation. The Czechoslovak government had already agreed to hand over the Sudetenland and now Beneš had the cheek to appoint a general as prime minister and mobilise the country's reservists. There was no mention of Hitler's new demands. The announcer was full of moral outrage: It is *essential* for the hand-over to be carried out *without delay*. If Beneš cannot keep his word, then his friends, the Western powers, should make him do so.

*

I can remember the days that followed almost hour by hour. Again, it was radio that defined the rhythm of events. On Monday 26th September, the world's eyes – or, more accurately, ears – were turned towards Berlin. Hitler was about to make a speech at the Sportpalast in Schöneberg. Bill Shirer was there for CBS, conjuring up the atmosphere in the hall for his listeners – the excited crowds and the slogans around the walls. *The Führer commands, we follow. Ein Volk. Ein Reich. Ein Führer.* He was fascinated by the circus that Goebbels had created around the event. Every radio station was to broadcast the gathering, and Shirer described the full-page ads in the German papers, telling people when and where to tune in. "Not a single person should fail to witness this historic event," they stated.

Not a single person. What a simple rule. If *everyone* hears, then it becomes truth, almost by definition. Shiela Grant Duff was right when she said that the Reich had become a world in itself.

*

And, of course, it was not just in Germany that people were listening. At Radiojournal, a couple of dozen journalists had gathered. Most of them were from the radio, but among them I also recognised Beuve-Méry from *Le Soir*, who was noisily threatening to leave his paper, if France carried on standing behind Chamberlain. The head of the French military mission in Czechoslovakia, General Faucher, had set a precedent three days before, resigning his commission and offering his services to Czechoslovakia.

We started by listening to Bill Shirer's commentary from the Sportpalast, but just before eight we switched directly to the Reichssender. We were just in time for the announcer to name excitedly the dozens of stations relaying the speech live ... "Argentina ... Denmark ... Finland ... Italy ... Japan ... Lithuania ... CBS with its hundred affiliates in the United States." In my mind I saw an American farmer, sitting on the veranda of his white clapboard house somewhere in the grain belt of the Midwest, enjoying a warm early autumn afternoon, his harvest safely collected and the radio buzzing in the background. Before long, Hitler began to speak and I wondered what the farmer would make of those alien cries in a distorted variant of a foreign language, a faraway world breaking into his home. I was sure that Mr Chamberlain in

London and Mr Daladier in Paris were also listening. They were hoping for a conciliatory tone from the German Chancellor.

As the speech went on, I tried to summarise Hitler's words for the foreign correspondents who did not speak German. What followed was a kind of pantomime, with Beneš the villain, whose very mention was greeted with jeers and mocking laughter, magnified fifteen thousand-fold. In my role as interpreter, I too began to feel like a pantomime figure.

The Czech state was built on a single lie ... *and the father of that lie was called Benesch!*

— loud jeers —

And the Anglo-Saxon statesmen, as always ill-informed on nationality issues, did not even deem it necessary to check these claims of Herr Benesch.

— contemptuous laughter —

In my interpreter's monotone, the straight-faced clown, I continued ...

Herr Benesch had established a tyrannical regime ... even the Slovaks didn't want to have anything more to do with the Czechs ... in the end England and France had accepted the only possible solution, that Czechoslovakia must be made to give up its German territory to the Reich.

The list of recriminations was winding up like a spring, and then released in the violent explosion of a single unfinished sentence.

This is the last territorial claim I have in Europe, but it is a claim that I shall never ...

And here the Führer's voice broke down into unintelligible syllables as the crowd burst into a prolonged roar.

There was nothing left to translate. I sat down, feeling as if Hitler's words had washed through me, stripping my bones bare.

Disman turned off the radio. Several people looked at one another, and after a while, someone said, "This means war".

I saw Mr Chamberlain in a comfortable armchair in his office in Downing Street. In the unseasonably cold weather that had settled over Europe, perhaps there was a fire burning in his grate. What images did he see dancing in the flames? And I saw my mother who would almost certainly be scribbling notes at home, huddled close to the wireless; she would be wondering how I would get back to London if war broke out.

"Hitler is like a wild animal," Robinson commented.

But Robinson was wrong, doing little service to the German Chancellor's art as a rhetorician. He had successfully transformed Beneš, the same sad Beneš who had addressed us in the rain two weeks before, into a demon hiding behind the mask of a technocrat.

"No." It was Jonathan Griffin who broke the long silence, "I do not think for a minute that this means war. You heard what Hitler just said – *this is the last territorial claim I have in Europe.* He hasn't said that before."

Griffin knew the situation in London better than any of us and had been concentrating on the Führer's every word. "It could be just what Chamberlain wants to hear. A promise of peace."

"But even Chamberlain must understand what utter nonsense that is," Beuve-Méry broke in. "Since when has any of Hitler's final demands been final? It's quite ..."

He hesitated as he looked for the word in English. Morrell finished for him

"... preposterous."

"I'm not so sure." Griffin seemed to be thinking things through as he spoke. "Chamberlain appears to trust Hitler, and we already know he is prepared to go to almost any length to prevent war. Can we really blame him? Aren't we all haunted by memories of the trenches? Aren't we now faced with something even more unthinkable, aerial bombardment that could wipe out our cities in days? I am not exaggerating. And what have we done to prepare ourselves, while Hitler has armed himself to the teeth?" He didn't wait for an answer. "France is even more paralysed than we are. And we should have no illusions. When it comes to it, Chamberlain and Daladier both prefer Herr Hitler to Comrade Stalin."

"A lovely pair," Jelínek muttered lugubriously. I wasn't quite sure whether he was talking about Hitler and Stalin or Chamberlain and Daladier.

We all went our separate ways. I walked alone down Wenceslas Square, which was very quiet and dark in the blackout, and across the river, back to Újezd. Even paní Lašková seemed to be sleeping. Before long, I too succumbed to the city's troubled sleep.

I was at a fairground in a rainstorm. I entered a red-and-white striped circus tent with stepped wooden seats around a ring with sawdust on the ground. In the middle was Hitler in uniform, delivering what seemed to be his Sportpalast speech into a microphone held in place by a spider's web of wires. I was the only other person in the tent. He began to dance and chant in staccato phrases ... *es hat sie keiner gefragt ... keiner ... hat ... sie ... gefragt ...* He was dancing with broad strides, sending up sawdust in little clouds. *Jeder hat ein Recht auf seinen Platz in der Sonne ... in der Sonne ...* Hip, hip, hooray! He burst into song again. The sun has got his hat on … I joined in, to a rhythm beaten out on the drums of a military band. He finished, bowed politely and I cheered wildly.

I woke up, heavy rain was falling outside.

*

In less than twenty-four hours, we were all back at Radio-journal – Morrell, the Griffins, Beuve-Méry and many from the radio itself, including Jelínek and Disman. Chamberlain was to make an address on the BBC. For the first time ever, the address was to be translated into French, German and Italian and broadcast on medium- and shortwave to Europe through the Empire Service. Reception was perfect. I had no need to translate this time. Chamberlain knew how to make himself understood.

With infinite politeness and poise, he began with an apology for not speaking earlier. For many in the room it was the first time they had heard Chamberlain's voice. He was speaking very slowly, the wise elder statesman, and what fascinated me most was his grasp of how radio worked. The lifelong amateur actor knew how to use the microphone, he knew that he could talk to each listener – intimately, one to one. I was enthralled by his mastery of the craft. This was far from the Commons, with its debating union banter. This was a play of emotions, and his words, rolling slowly off his tongue, were addressed above all to women.

First of all, I must say something to those who have written to my wife or myself in these last weeks to tell us of their gratitude for my efforts and to assure us of their prayers for my success. Most of these letters have come from women – mothers or sisters of our own countrymen. But there are countless others

*besides – from France, from Belgium, from Italy, and even from
Germany, and it has been heart-breaking to read the growing
anxiety they reveal and their intense relief when they thought,
too soon, that the danger of war was past.*

*If I felt my responsibility heavy before, to read such letters
has made it seem almost overwhelming.*

Almost overwhelming. His words had become thick and heavy.
The actor Petr Lotar walked into the room and stopped dead.
He had happened to be in the broadcasting house to rehearse
for a radio play and had heard that a group of us were listening to the speech. "Is that him … Chamberlain?" He nodded
towards the radio. "That old man?" After a while he added,
"That voice seeps into your body like lead."

*How horrible, fantastic, incredible it is that we should be
digging trenches and trying on gas-masks here because of a
quarrel in a far-away country between people of whom we
know nothing. It seems still more impossible that a quarrel
which has already been settled in principle should be the
subject of war.*

At that moment, Bill Morrell leapt up, waving wildly at the big
radio set like Don Quixote tilting at windmills.

"You do not describe your allies as a people of whom you
know nothing." He fumed. "You bang the drum and blow the
trumpet in a million ways... A million subtle ways," he added,
calming a little.

Quite unmoved by the untimely interruption, the radio
went on.

*I can well understand the reasons why the Czech Government
have felt unable to accept the terms which have been put before
them in the German memorandum. Yet I believe after my talks
with Herr Hitler that, if only time were allowed, it ought to be
possible for the arrangements for transferring the territory that
the Czech Government has agreed to give to Germany to be
settled by agreement under conditions which would assure fair
treatment to the population concerned.*

*You know already that I have done all that one man can
do to compose this quarrel. After my visits to Germany I have
realised vividly how Herr Hitler feels that he must champion
other Germans, and his indignation that grievances have not
been met before this. He told me privately, and last night he
repeated publicly, that after this Sudeten German question
is settled, that is the end of Germany's territorial claims in
Europe.*

*However much we may sympathise with a small nation
confronted by a big and powerful neighbour, we cannot in all
circumstances undertake to involve the whole British Empire
in war simply on her account. If we have to fight it must be on
larger issues than that.*

At the words *on larger issues than that,* Bill Morrell walked out
of the room.

"Apparently the British Prime Minister is becoming so popular in Germany that Hitler is beginning to be jealous," Jelínek
remarked at the end of the speech and Joan Griffin added, "The
German people probably don't want war any more than anyone
else, but Hitler certainly does. Chamberlain's success is built on

giving Hitler, step by step, everything he wants, so that Hitler runs out of reasons for war."

In his broadcast, Chamberlain had promised to work for peace to the last moment, and that is just what he did. How he turned his third and final trip to Germany into a spectacular diplomatic triumph after all the pessimism of the days before was nothing short of alchemy. Lead was turned to gold, Petr Lotar might have said.

*

My mother sent me a letter on the 29th of September, the day that Chamberlain left for Munich. She wrote with her typical mixture of tenderness and documentary detachment. I have kept it, in a bundle with her other letters from the time, and now I am reading it again for the first time in over fifty years.

> … As I write this, it seems that we are at peace, at least for the time being. I pray that my letter will reach you. Everything has been moving so fast. After Hitler's speech in Berlin on Monday, we all felt that war could break out at any moment. I was so afraid for you, wondering how you would get out of Czechoslovakia. And here in Britain all the talk has been of air raids. Yesterday's papers carried headlines about the mobilisation of the fleet and the BBC has been telling us not to hoard food. I am praying for peace and more than anything else I am thinking of your safety.
>
> On Wednesday, there was still no news from Berlin and we all waited for Mr Chamberlain's address to parliament. Apparently, there were plans for it to go out on the wireless – it is amazing to think of a debate in parliament being brought to us through our

*radio sets. Do you remember how I took you to the Commons
once as a little boy and you laughed that the MPs reminded you
of the sheep on the Thames marshes with their muttering and
their "Hear, hears!"? Anyway, in the end they decided not to
broadcast the debate. I am not sure why. It's a shame, because
today's papers report that it was all quite dramatic. In the middle
of the Prime Minister's speech, he was interrupted. Someone
handed him a note, telling him that Herr Hitler had agreed to
meet him in Munich and postpone the German mobilisation
by twenty-four hours. There were cheers for Mr Chamberlain,
and, I'm told, also for Mr Mussolini, whom the Prime Minister
thanked for being willing to work with us for peace in Europe.
The whole thing ended with a prolonged roar and a storm of
order papers being waved. Apparently even the Archbishop of
Canterbury was cheering. But I expect that by now you will have
read about all this as well. It's strange how everyone has stopped
talking about Czechoslovakia itself, but perhaps it is good for
Prague to be out of the spotlight.*

*I have just heard on the wireless that a large delegation has
assembled at Downing Street and Chamberlain is set to fly
to Munich. The whole mood has changed here. There's a sense
of relief, although goodness only knows how long it will last.
Apparently, the PM will be giving another statement at Heston
Aerodrome before he takes off, so I'll quickly put this letter in the
post, and try to get back to listen. By the time you read this, I
expect he will be back in London. Anna and I are hoping and
praying that all will be well and that we shall see you soon.*

*Líbám Tě
Máma*

In the Spirit of Saint Wenceslas

Father Reichenberger came to my rooms in Újezd. The Pope was to give an address on Vatican Radio about the Czechoslovak crisis and I had invited the Father to join me. My radio, which I had shipped over from England in a crate, much to the amusement of my Czech friends, could pick up just about any signal making its way back to earth from the ionosphere, and after a bit of tinkering with the antenna, we managed to get an audible signal from Rome. Father Reichenberger was pacing up and down the room, even more nervous than the last time we had met. As I fiddled with the dial, he sat down, and began stroking his beard absently. "A week ago I still felt some hope." He spoke quietly, while snatches of choral music drifted from the radio, coming and going with the static. "When Henlein and his people ran off, everything suddenly felt better. Somehow the pressure had gone and for the first time in nearly a year there was a hint of normality. But that is over now. I fear that Czechoslovakia is lost. Do you think the people in London and Paris know what they are doing?"

I began to feel as nervous as my companion.

"Members of my congregation, people I've known for thirty years and whose children and grandchildren I've baptised, cross the street to avoid me. On Sunday only one person turned up for Mass, an old man who took me by both hands and begged me to leave, to find somewhere safe, away from the Sudetenland. At first I could hardly grasp what he was saying. Am I to become an exile in my own land?"

The music stopped. The Holy Father was announced. Father Reichenberger stood up, crossed himself, walked a couple of times agitatedly around the room and sat down again. The words were hardly decipherable, but after a while, the message became clear enough, even in Italian. The Czech translation that followed confirmed my impression. The Pope was appealing for peace and for all channels of communication to remain open. That went without saying. But above all he called on Czechs to act in the spirit of the Patron of Bohemia, Saint Wenceslas, the Good King of the carol. Wenceslas was the prince who, a thousand years ago, had made peace with the neighbouring German tribes. Now it was up to the Czechs to do the same again. The message was unambiguous. It was the Czechs and the Czechs alone who bore the moral responsibility for pre-venting catastrophe.

Father Reichenberger left as soon as the broadcast was over. He did not say a word and I am not sure he could have spoken if he had tried. I watched through the dusty glass of my little window as he walked slowly and stooping down the cobbled lane towards the main road. He had seen his world crumble. Germany had turned its back on all he believed in, then it was the turn of the Sudeten politicians, followed, in confusion, by his own congregation; he had seen Runciman and Chamberlain embrace the most aggressive German nationalists, he had been snubbed by the Czechoslovak government – even they preferred to negotiate with Henlein – and had been spat upon by people calling themselves Czech patriots. Now we were hearing the same from the Holy Father himself, whose portrait I had seen hanging protectively above his desk in the Wiese presbytery. *We stand on the edge of a precipice...* I recalled the apocalyptic words with which Father Reichenberger had opened his talk in the Radiojournal studio ... *A dance of death is due to begin.*

*

I tried to follow Chamberlain's departure for Munich on the radio, but the signal remained weak. Shortwave reception had been poor for some days because of solar radiation in the upper ionosphere. Perhaps Apollo was playing his part in a malign conspiracy. The cheers of the enthusiastic crowd at Heston Aerodrome melted into static. I switched to medium wave, where reception was far better and a couple of hours later I caught the German reports of the arrival of Chamberlain's big silver Lockheed 14 at Oberwiesenfeld in Munich. The cheers of the crowd almost drowned out the roar of the plane. Then a German military band hammered out God Save the King which faded seamlessly into the anthem of the Nazi Party, the *Horst Wessel Lied.*

As Hitler, Mussolini, Daladier and Chamberlain gathered at the Führerbau in Munich, a solitary figure was walking up the stairs of the broadcasting house in Fochova Street with slow deliberate steps, carrying just a sheet of paper. It was Professor Jan Slavík. With Gordon Skilling I had attended several of his public lectures on European history and I wondered if it was Skilling who had invited him to the radio now. He was to deliver a short talk for Radiojournal. Slavík's views of history were unfashionable. When it came to historical truth, he said, no one could claim the final word. There was no nugget waiting to be found and drawn from the murk of the past. History was real enough, but it reflected the age in which it was being told and those who were telling it. He was deeply suspicious of the national versions of European history to which politicians were trying to make our battered and confused continent fit. His talk was sober, clear and, at that moment, heretical.

> *The opinions are being voiced today that Germany is fighting for the right of self-determination for the German people. They have to be answered as follows. He has no right to expound these high principles who is treading on them by the theory of the supremacy of his race, by his theories of master and slave nations. Those who want to make use of the right to self-determination against us have no moral right to do so, until they proclaim before the whole world the principle that they recognise the equality of all nations as well as their right to live. Until they disclaim the programme of violent conquest of the territories of other European nations, as it is outlined in Adolf Hitler's book* My Struggle, *their excited shouting about the rights of their nation remains a mere sound.*

A mere sound from which weapons were being forged. All sides must have been only too aware of the double standard to which Professor Slavík was referring, but what mattered were the guns and tanks from which words, forged into shells, could be fired.

At the end of Slavík's talk it was announced that it would be followed by an English translation on Radiojournal's shortwave service.

In the Führerbau, Hitler, Mussolini, Chamberlain and Daladier sat down to talks with Slavík's words hovering unheard in the air. No amount of alchemy would turn his words into shells and no one in that little group had any interest in listening. Even if, for some unlikely reason, Mr Chamberlain or Mr Daladier had chosen to tune into the wireless in their hotel rooms, to catch Radiojournal during a break in the negotiations, they would have been breaking the law. In Germany there were heavy penalties for listening to foreign wireless stations.

A little after midnight, the Munich Agreement was signed. To all intents and purposes, Czechoslovakia had ceased to exist.

The Stones Themselves Will Cry

'Off with his head!' she said, without even looking round.

By mid-morning, the events in Munich were common knowledge in Prague. There was no official announcement, just rumour and the reports coming from the German wireless stations.

For no particular reason I wandered up to the British Embassy, where an extra policeman had been put on duty in case of any spontaneous expressions of anger. After showing one of the policemen my British passport, I hesitated before ringing the bell. What would I say? Who would I ask for? Instead I walked back to Újezd, and, by habit as much as intention, switched the radio to the BBC. Britain was putting out the flags. War had been avoided, and Mr Chamberlain was the hero of the day. In the early afternoon Chamberlain's plane landed back in London. The BBC announcer commented excitedly that for the first time ever, television cameras were capturing a news event live. As I listened I tried to imagine the magical flickering images.

This time the plane doors opened without difficulty; the Prime Minister climbed down the steps and spoke. In the last weeks I had got used to all kinds of political sleight of hand, but now, by the most extraordinary conjuring trick, a whole country was made to disappear. Of the agreement to dissect Czechoslovakia that he had signed in Munich a few hours before there was no mention. Instead there was another document to talk about, simple and just fifteen lines long, signed by Herr Hitler and Mr Chamberlain, and no one besides, a pact of non-aggression between the Reich and the British Empire, a promise of peace. Several times I heard the microphone catch the piece of paper as Chamberlain waved it in the air. At no point was Czechoslovakia even named. I was listening from a place that did not exist.

> `That is not said right,' said the Caterpillar.
> `Not QUITE right, I'm afraid,' said Alice, timidly; some of the words have got altered.'

*

I walked to Wenceslas Square. Again a crowd had gathered, but it was quite silent. Some had tears in their eyes. People were moving backwards and forwards, without words. As I arrived in Fochova Street, a number of government limousines pulled up, discreetly, without flags. I noticed General Syrový with his eye patch, and ministers Hugo Vavrečka and Ivan Dérer, along with the chief-of-staff Ludvík Krejčí.

Vavrečka's daughter Božena Havlová was standing by the entrance to the radio waiting for her father. I had met her once before at the British Embassy with her brother-in-law, the film magnate Miloš Havel. We stood and talked for a while. She was heavily pregnant and was holding a little boy's hand. "Vašek will be two next week," she said, roughing his hair as the rather shy little boy poked his head quizzically round her skirt. Božena's father was the propaganda minister, a post that had only just been thought up as a desperate response to what was going on in Germany, but he was an unlikely candidate for the job, a thoughtful democrat with dreams of a Europe without borders.

"What a time to be bringing children into the world," Božena hugged her son affectionately. I wanted to say something cheering, but words failed me. As I went through the glass doors, which were still cracked after the events of a week before, Vašek stuck out his tongue at me. "Rascal," I smiled back and ran up the stairs, nearly bumping into a sound engineer coming down. My apology came out as a croak. I had lost my voice, suddenly and unexpectedly.

In the studio Prime Minister Syrový had already begun to speak, to address the nation. Repeatedly he appealed to citizens to remain calm, but his words were quite superfluous. The entire country was becalmed. Vavrečka talked about Europe, about the allies, Britain and France, without whom Czechoslovakia could do nothing. He had his usual patiently courteous tone, weighing each word. He did not sound bitter, but his words were of betrayal.

Vavrečka was followed by the justice minister, the Slovak Social Democrat Ivan Dérer. Behind the glass he looked like a caged animal. He was a tough man, a war veteran and an old friend of President Masaryk, but now he was having difficulty controlling his voice. Several times he fell quite silent. He broke into sobs, shaking violently, as he spoke of what could have happened if Czechoslovakia had decided to fight alone, "Our friends to the west would have decided it is a battle of communism against western civilization." Could he be right, as Morrell had recently warned? Had everything been turned so completely on its head that Britain would consider taking sides with Hitler against Beneš? His voice broke down again, sobs overwhelming him in waves. "We had to choose. Either a war, a heroic struggle by our armed forces, but a struggle without hope ... " He leapt an octave, "a war ... which would have ended not just with the destruction of our brave troops ... but with our nation being quite wiped out ... with the murder of our mothers, women and children ... " By now he was weeping openly. The studio engineer looked at us for help, not sure whether to keep the justice minister on air. We all looked to the ground.

It was already late into the evening. Trams had long stopped running and I walked home. Few people were outside, just occasional groups of policemen with nothing to do. Ever since the mobilisation had been announced a week earlier, there had been almost no cars, and Prague remained under a fairy-tale spell. The beauty of the Old Town was almost unbearably painful. The Vltava flowed on apathetically and as I crossed the Charles Bridge the verse from the Gospel came to my mind – *If the people fail to speak, the stones themselves will cry out.* But no stones cried out. Even the statues of the Saints remained mendaciously silent.

Nothing had been signed or stated to the effect, technically this was just a change of border, but, like everyone else, I knew that Masaryk's republic had ended, and God only knew what would come in its place. Back in my flat, I collapsed onto my bed without even taking off my boots and switched on the radio. It was a church service from London, to give thanks for the peace that had been secured.

The German Motor Train

The Hotel Ambassador over breakfast was filled with suitcases. The crisis was over and the world's reporters were leaving. Czechoslovakia had become yesterday's story and soon would disappear from the bulletins altogether. Even so, a small group had gathered in the corner, hoping to go to Carlsbad, to report on the Führer's triumphant arrival. I croaked and gesticulated that I had lost my voice …

Eleanor Whitmore swept into the room theatrically. She looked outraged.

Bill Morrell called over to her. "Are you joining us?"

"Ha. Thought I was but … look at this … "

She waved a telegram in the air … laughing contemptuously, "I have in my hand a piece of paper."

The other journalists cheered mockingly and one of them broke into song,

God bless you, Mr Chamberlain,
We're all mighty proud of you.

Everyone joined in, although I could only mime the words

You look swell with your umb-er-ella,
All the world loves a wonderful fella …

"It's from my editor. The story's done, stop, readers have had enough, stop, come home, stop."

And before long we found it was the same with most of the news people around us. There was to be no war, and this was yesterday's story. Only a handful of us, Bill Morrell, his colleague from the *Express* Geoffrey Cox and myself headed to Carlsbad, with Vincent Sheean from the *New York Herald Tribune* driving us in his car with GB plates. Without a voice, I would not be much use as an interpreter, but no one seemed to mind.

A few miles before Carlsbad we spotted the first swastika, waving from the barn of a hillside farmhouse. The Czech troops we encountered, travelling the other way, looked quite different from the soldiers we had seen in Prague after the mobilisation a few days before. They were dishevelled, hunched, some absent-mindedly biting at a roll or drinking from a tin mug, all quite silent. Beaten without having fought, Sheean remarked. A couple of times we came across trucks with tarpaulins, or horse-drawn wagons, sometimes several dozen at a time. Refugees. As we entered the town, some people noticed the British number plates. They cheered loudly, many raising their right hand with *Heil Hitler* and shouting thanks to Chamberlain. Sheean noticed the Jewish charity hospital, carefully boarded up, and, nearby, what had been a Jewish old-people's home. A swastika was hanging from it. I wondered about the people who had lived there. We ended up at the Hotel Goldenes Schild, which I had visited with Morrell just a couple of weeks before. No sign of our nervous Czech waiter now. Instead, looking out over a Pilsner beer, we were witnesses to a peculiar theatre. A regiment of men, women and children had appeared from nowhere. They were uprooting all the plants, trees and rosebushes in the Municipal Gardens. It all looked too disciplined to be mere looting. Then we caught sight of several German officers in the square. This strange regiment was making room for the crowds to be addressed by the Führer.

We joined them, standing as close to the platform as we could get. It gave us the chance to see Dr Goebbels' propaganda machine in action, a thing called the German Motor Train. This consisted of a whole busload of big loud speakers which were being fixed all over the town, a diesel-driven dynamo car, a wireless outside broadcast car, a platform on wheels for cinema operators, microphones and cables. Half a dozen five-ton vans. And with it numerous officials of the Propaganda Ministry and official journalists in brown uniforms. When all was set up, they sat and rested, and all wrote postcards home to commemorate the day.

*

Sieg Heil. The crowd cheered. The Führer had arrived. Brusque, businesslike, without further ado, he began his speech. Short and to the point.

"At last, irrevocably and for all eternity this land has become a part of the Reich of the German nation. We shall never leave this place again. Now I can say it openly. On the morning of the 2nd October we would have marched into this land come what may."

To all appearances the Führer was much disappointed at not being allowed to have his war. In one voice the crowd thanked their leader. We felt conspicuous, standing by the podium in silence. I pretended to be taking copious notes. Henlein spoke, the same Henlein I remembered from Breslau. But now the future he had spoken of then was no longer a dream. He did not rage against the Czechs, or even the western statesmen. His enemy was closer to home.

"At those times, when we were fighting for our freedom and our future, there were some people willing to take up arms and use them against their own blood brothers. A Marxist mob. This Marxist mob raped and pillaged in our land. And when they understood that Germany meant things seriously, most of them just ran away. But now the Czechs are cheerfully sending these German-speaking Marxists back to our country. I state categorically that these people have no right to forgiveness."

The crowd burst into laughter.

"And we shall grant them no forgiveness. I intend to have them locked up until they rot. And some of them are now considering coming back of their own accord to the Sudetenland, to see if it might just be possible to live here …"

There was more mocking laughter.

"And I say to them, do not dare to take even one step into our homeland."

*

Back in Prague there were ever more refugees in the streets. This time they were Czechs who had fled the Sudetenland. Perhaps there were some Germans among them, but they did not risk speaking German in public for fear of being sent back. The Central Europe of different nations and tongues had disappeared overnight, and in Prague too there was an undercurrent of something new, indefinable but menacing enough. Sympathy for Sudeten refugees had been replaced with nervous suspicion. At the radio headquarters I found several colleagues who happened to be Jewish getting ready to leave; apparently the radio director Šourek had spoken of the importance of not provoking the Germans. In fury, Gordon Skilling handed in his resignation, and there was a rumour that one old general had gone down to the Vltava and tossed away his French *Légion d'Honneur*. The mood was sober and the sense of bitter disillusionment with Beneš and Masaryk's republic was palpable in every conversation.

President Beneš resigned, with the same courteous, quietly recriminating sadness that I had heard from Hugo Vavrečka. One day history would judge these events, he said, and then was silent. The crowds of foreign journalists left Prague to its fate and the radio building became eerily quiet.

A few did remain. Joan and Jonathan Griffin were in no hurry to leave; they had their book to finish and they felt it was more urgent than ever to record the consequences of what Joan called the vivisection of Czechoslovakia. Ivan Jelínek commissioned them to give a series of talks for Radiojournal's English service, relating developments step by step. It went without saying that this was behind Šourek's back. Jonathan described the atmosphere in the streets of Prague, the clusters of people gathering anxiously around maps that had been hurriedly pasted in shop windows as the new borders were drawn; he spoke of the eerie calm, no panic, no shortages and no spontaneous outrage; just a deep sadness as winter gradually fell on the city.

I was following developments from bed. I could not shake off a high fever and my voice refused to return. I felt a little self-conscious when the Griffins came to see me in my shabby rooms; both stooping like giants under the low ceilings. Jonathan joked that it was refreshing to visit someone who could not answer back, "rather a good secret weapon," and Joan showed me an article from *The Times* about how Czechoslovakia would now be free to develop, *smaller and happier because homogenous.*

"Can they mean this seriously?" She was indignant. "How can a democracy thrive – or even survive – surrounded by the most aggressive dictatorships imaginable?" As they parted, Jonathan speculated what would happen if Hitler were to lose his voice. "It would be a bit like Čapek's *White Disease*. Perhaps silence is the greatest weapon of all." I smiled politely, glad that they had come, but relieved when they left.

In the end I was admitted to the hospital near Charles Square. My temperature fell quickly, but I remained weak and unable to speak. The doctors were baffled, but when Ivan Jelínek came to see me he was not surprised in the least.

"What do you expect? You have run out of words. You have been doing the impossible – you are an *interpreter* but you have been interpreting things that cannot be interpreted. It is quite simply too much and you have lost yourself. Quite logical really. Silence prevails!"

This time it was Ivan who quoted from Alice in Wonderland.

'What do you mean by that?' said the Caterpillar sternly. 'Explain yourself!'

'I can't explain myself, I'm afraid, sir' said Alice, 'because I'm not myself, you see.'

I smiled back and looked out of the window. I realised how much I was going to miss Jelínek once I left this country. By now the leaves were beginning to turn, and in the distance a train was crossing the Vltava. It was almost a year ago that I had accompanied Ivan on my first visit to Radiojournal and been taken aback by the irony with which he had uttered the words "Truth will prevail." Now it was clear. Ivan read my thoughts and, as he had done during our first meeting in U Kocoura, he set about raising my spirits. He turned back as he left the ward and smiled broadly, "We shall speak of books; once again the world will be filled with life."

"František Halas," I mimed, recognising the quote, but without a voice. He went out into the corridor and in a few seconds I heard his light steps on the stairs.

*

I did get to speak of books with Ivan, but it was not for several years, and never again in Prague.

When some of my strength had returned I was released from hospital.

I opened the low front door of the little house in Újezd. There was no hallway, just a dank vaulted passage leading into the tiny courtyard, and, on the right, a row of rusting letter-boxes. A letter had arrived from my mother, and once I reached the half-light of the courtyard I could make out the date on the postmark, September 29th. There was also a note from Ilse, saying that she had dropped by. It was in Czech and dated October 10th, already ten days old. I put the heavy key of my rooms back into my pocket and made for Karlín. The plants on the little landing where Peter had hidden on my first visit had wilted, and it was clear that no one was living in the little flat. "They've gone abroad," a neighbour whispered cautiously through an open window onto the courtyard. I walked home via Wilson Station and bought a ticket to London, communicating through notes and gestures, my voice still showing no sign of returning. I sent a telegram to my mother, telling her that I was heading home and two days later I was on my way.

Four months later German troops marched into Prague.

The journey through Germany and the Netherlands was grey and desolate. At the Hook of Holland I took the ferry to Harwich and then another train to Liverpool Street on the eastern edge of the City of London. In the coming months many refugees from Germany and Czechoslovakia were to follow this same route, people who left all but their lives behind. For me it was easier. My mother and Anna were waiting at the platform and we walked home hand in hand through the shabby, reassuring streets in which I had grown up. My trunk arrived the next day, along with my boxed-up wireless set, and I went back to the station to pick them up.

I continued to convalesce gradually. I remained virtually unable to speak for nearly three years, much to the fascination of various London specialists, none of whom was able to offer an explanation more convincing than the one proposed by Ivan

Jelínek. I became more introverted, preferring to communicate through letters.

When the war came, I was ruled out for military service, although I was quite fit apart from my voice. I had kept in touch with Joan and Jonathan Griffin, and they would write to me from time to time, usually to ask about the meaning of some word or phrase in Czech or German. Their book about the events in Czechoslovakia came out early in 1939 and was an instant bestseller. The euphoria of Munich had taken no more than two or three months to dissipate as its consequences became clear and war loomed. Jonathan was put in charge of European Intelligence at the BBC, and it was through his influence that I was given work at the BBC monitoring service in Evesham.

We worked from a rambling nineteenth century country house that had once been the home of the last pretender to the French throne, the Duc d'Orléans and still bore his monogram in the woodwork above the fireplaces, on the banisters and even on the light switches. It sounds rather grand but I was billeted along with several others in a tiny cottage that could hardly have been more basic. There was not even a fireplace in my room and on cold winter mornings the window would be opaque with ice. The cottage belonged to a market gardener, who never stopped complaining about being told by the government what to grow. Ewald, a young man from Prague of about my age, billeted in the room next to mine, was shocked at this lack of patriotism and I thought he was going to explode when our landlord suggested that when the Germans came, even they would need feeding.

Our work was supposed to be secret and this only heightened the suspicion of local people, not helped by the fact that many of the monitors were decidedly foreign in their accents and peculiar habits. There were so many different native tongues that I lost count. Many of my colleagues were Jewish and I soon realised that they included some of Europe's most distinguished linguists. Ewald, who picked up languages as the rest of us picked up colds during the damp winters, was in his element. During long evenings, with no entertainment beyond melancholy walks in the country or occasional trips to the pub in Wood Norton, he was often at the centre of lively discussions about poetry and translation. One evening he organised a competition to translate some of Petrarch's sonnets. We all took it very seriously indeed.

But this was no ivory tower. Nearly all the refugees had disturbing stories to tell of how they came to be here, and the reality of the war never seemed far away.

I was part of a small team monitoring broadcasts in Czech and German from the "Reich Protectorate of Bohemia and Moravia": for eight hours every day I would be quite immersed in a world that I saw being transformed step by step into an experimental Gestapo state that preserved an almost perfect illusion of order and decorum. At the end of my shift, I would remove my headphones, leave occupied Prague for an English country estate surrounded by cabbage fields and water meadows, and it would fade like a nightmare.

So Alice sat on with closed eyes, and half believed herself in Wonderland.

From the Island

Ivan Jelínek also reached Britain, but not until 1940, via Yugoslavia and then France. One day, in the summer of 1941, I received a letter from the Isle of Man, marked with a military censor's stamp. It was from Ilse and was written in flawless English.

My Friend,

You are perhaps surprised to receive a letter from such an unlikely address. I am in a detention camp for enemy aliens. I do not feel like an enemy or an alien, but last year I was sent here together with Peter. Up to that time we had been in Manchester. Together with Uncle Emmanuel we managed to get to Britain through his contacts in the Catholic Church. That was just after the annexation of the Sudetenland. It was awfully complicated. The Czechs saw us as unwanted foreigners and I need not tell you what they thought of us in Germany.

It's also thanks to Mr Chamberlain's Munich Agreement that I ended up here in the camp. Since I was born in Liberec, which is now in the Reich, I am treated as a Reich German and not a Czechoslovak refugee. I hope the censor will forgive me, but the Home Office is almost as fond of categories as Herr Hitler. They have put me in Class B. That means I am an alien of questionable loyalty.

There are some three thousand women here in the camp, many of them Jewish. The other day I found myself talking about Prague with a woman I met in the washhouse and she turned out to be Dora Diamant. Do you remember her? Her husband was the editor of the Communist paper, Die Rote Fahne. I didn't dare ask what has happened to him. I've just heard that she is going to be released in a few days. I shouldn't say so, but it made me a little sad. I'd love to get to know her more. Did you know that she was with Franz Kafka when he died in Austria? Apparently he spent his last moments in her arms. That reminds me – I once had a big argument with Uncle Emmanuel about Kafka. Uncle didn't like his stories. He said they were the product of his rootless Jewish cosmopolitanism and had nothing to do with our Christian world. I didn't talk to him for two months after that. Now Emmanuel is uprooted too. He's in America, on the invitation of the Kolping House in Chicago and is living on the edge of an Indian settlement, thirty miles from the nearest small town. He was never one to do things in half measures and it seems that he actually chose to be sent there by the church. Perhaps he is punishing himself, but I don't know what for.

To be quite honest I fear that events have broken his heart. Although he doesn't say so directly, I think he feels desperately lonely and abandoned. Here at least I have Peter. He's awfully affected by the anti-German feeling around him and has been writing lots of articles to try to persuade people that Germany isn't just the Nazis. But I fear he's like Don Quixote and his windmills. To be quite honest, with the war raging you can't really be surprised how people feel. In fact, it's one of the reasons why I almost feel relieved to be here in the camp. At least we're all in the same boat here.

Some have managed to get out through political or other connections, and I've been told I could probably do the same with a bit of help from the Catholic Church. But when it comes to it, I think I would rather stay. I was never much of a good Catholic anyway. We are far from the war here and Peter has grown to like it. We are used to the wide grey sea and the ever-changing clouds. I feel sorry that we are not allowed down to the beach – it has been mined in case of invasion, or perhaps in case we try to escape! (forgive me, censor, I don't mean it). I would love to swim among the waves. The Ilse of Man – that's what they call me here. Oh, the English and their puns!

I hope that you and your mother and sister have managed to keep well away from all the bombs that are falling on London. I read that the East End has suffered most. Strange how it is always the poor who are worst hit.

I found out about your illness by chance. When we got our visas we had to leave quickly, but I wanted to say goodbye. I came round to Újezd and the old seamstress who lives in the room opposite paní Lašková told me you were in hospital. She didn't know which one. And as I left, paní Lašková asked me the time… Morning or evening? I hope the Protectorate has left her untouched.

I have thought of you often. Do write.

Ilse

We wrote to each other a few more times during the war. In the isolation of the monitoring station in Evesham I looked forward hugely to Ilse's letters. In one she joked that I should marry her, that it would be a way for her to leave the camp.

The war ended and I felt emptiness rather than euphoria. I tried to find out more about my old friends from Prague. Franta Kocourek, one of the star reporters from Radiojournal had been murdered in Auschwitz, as had the announcer Zdenka Walló. I can still see her vividly, calling Professor Einstein from the radio studio and beaming as director Šourek congratulates her. František Kraus from the English service survived Auschwitz and other camps. Just after the war I was sent a piece he had written, on how, in June 1942, together with other prisoners in the Terezín Ghetto, he had been forced to bury the 173 men shot by the SS in Lidice. His style was precise and unadorned, although the dreadfulness of what it was describing made it seem surreal. The discipline of his profession as a journalist had not abandoned him even as he described the unthinkable. Reading the piece reminded me again of the oddly civilised hell that I had encountered every day as I monitored the sounds of the Protectorate. Miloslav Disman somehow survived the war in Prague. I do not know how. I have no idea what became of Oswald Bamborough or Wilfred Robinson. I would love to travel back in time and sit with the two of them again in a noisy Prague pub. Shiela Grant Duff became the first Czechoslovak editor in the European Service of the BBC, and Bill Morrell had an adventurous war. As a Special Operations Executive agent, he was sent to the Middle East. I imagine him in some dangerous operation together with his trusty terrier

Pop, the hero of a schoolboy adventure. He survived and I believe he moved to America. Ivan Jelínek is at the BBC. We meet from time to time.

*

Once, just after the war, I saw Ilse again. She wrote that she was living near London and had recently married. I took the train to an industrial town on the wide Essex marshes and knocked on the door of a small newly built terraced house. It was a windy spring morning, with clouds scurrying over the cranes in the Thames Estuary. Her husband was not at home; he worked at the nearby car factory, and I was relieved to be spared all those polite English introductions. Ilse was six months pregnant and Peter was a tall twelve-year-old English lad, with no recollections of Prague. The two of them chatted in English and it seemed quite natural that Ilse and I should speak English too. She was obviously quite at home and had changed little, despite the move to another country and another language. We drank tea the English way with milk in the little living room which was clean, new and sparsely furnished, and we reminisced about Prague. I asked about Father Reichenberger. He was still in America but she said that his letters had become fewer, increasingly distant and distracted. "He longs to be back home, but I fear that the home he dreams of is just in his head. He is even thinking of moving to Germany, but I don't think it would be a good idea. You know, the home he lost cannot be found on any map."

After a couple of hours we said goodbye. Ilse waved from the tiny front garden, with a sad and slightly concerned smile, as if she were afraid for me. I had recognised the same smile when she had talked about Father Reichenberger. The train took me home through the bomb-scarred landscape of east London and I felt quite alone.

Our Father

Nuremberg, August 1950

On Nuremberg's market square, the Hauptmarkt, I stopped short. Outside the west porch of the Frauenkirche, still a shell, clad in scaffolding and casting sharp shadows in the hot afternoon sunshine, there was a small table. It was laden with books for sale, most of them on religious subjects. One bore the title *Ostdeutsche Passion*; on the cover was a woodcut: an endless column of people, their heads bowed low, a great cross hovering above them, as if they were bearing it collectively to Calvary. The author: Father E.J. Reichenberger.

The face of the elderly woman behind the stall lit up. "Our Father – the Father of the Expelled," she said reverently. She handed me another book by the same E.J. Reichenberger. It had just come out, *Europe in Ruins – the Outcome of the Allies' Crusade*. I bought both books and carried them through the building sites and neat piles of rubble back to my hotel. As I walked away, the old woman told me that Father Reichenberger would be holding a special mass here on the square on Sunday morning.

Back in my hotel I leafed through the books. In America, Reichenberger had missed the horrors of the war but the books were not about the war. They were about the fate of Sudeten Germans forced to leave Czechoslovakia after the war had ended.

*

Several hundred people of all generations gathered on the Hauptmarkt to attend the mass and listen to the *Father* – as everyone called him, using the English word. As soon as he climbed onto the wooden stage in front of the church, I recognised his neatly trimmed pointed beard, now almost white. I worked out that he must now be in his mid-sixties. Flanked by two younger priests, he started with a blessing and a prayer, and I recalled the service in Wiese over a decade before, amid the spring meadows of North Bohemia.

The sermon was about suffering.

"... Let me tell you what happened to Helene. Twenty women, some in their sixties and seventies were handed over to the hate-filled mass of people. Under a constant battering of truncheons and sticks Helene could just hear the order, 'Kneel down, you German whores!'"

"Ihr deutsche Huren ... " These last words echoed round the square. The Father spoke slowly, deliberately, just as I remembered from before the war.

"The twenty women kneeled down. The men hacked at their hair using their bayonets. Helene fell unconscious and was brought round with ice-cold water. Some of her fellow sufferers were lying around her, their limbs stiff, they were already dead …

This was the true genocide of the war."

He recounted several harrowing stories in succession and it was clear that he was not talking of these events for the first time. Some I could remember from the two books I had glanced at the night before. He spoke of Czechoslovakia with an unconcealed bitterness. The crowd on the square looked tired, troubled, many of them in ill-fitting, worn clothes. Some seemed transfixed, others distracted. I remembered the words of his radio talk from before the war, warning of a dance of death that was about to break out. Were these the exhausted dying steps of that same dance? At that time, many Sudeten Germans had despised him. Now he was seen as their Father. Outwardly, he had changed little, yet in his words I did not recognise the parish priest of Wiese. A couple of American soldiers stood, rather bored, on the far corner of the square, watching proceedings. At the end of the service people flocked around the Father. I waited for around twenty minutes before I approached him. For a moment he looked bewildered, as if I had come from a different world – and at that moment I felt that I had – but then he recognised me and shook my hand warmly. We arranged to meet the next day at my hotel.

*

It was a bright morning, but the sharp sunlight only seemed to heighten the soullessness of the hotel's surroundings. Father Reichenberger arrived exactly on time. I offered him tea or coffee in the hotel, but the place was so impersonal and utilitarian that we decided on a walk instead. Something led us in the direction of the lake, the Dutzendteich. The Father seemed subdued, but when we talked about Ilse, his spirits rose, and still more when I told him that I had been to see her and that she had seemed happy. He was uncomfortable talking about the time before the war and instead gave me details of his work with Sudeten German refugees, how he was helping them to find somewhere to live or work or just to find lost relatives. He spoke at some length, returning repeatedly to accounts of the refugees' suffering at the hands of the Czech military, the police and civilians. He repeated the word "Czech" frequently, always with bitterness. in a few words I told him about my wartime work at the monitoring station.

We reached the lake and continued in silence, eventually stopping to look across at the former Parteigelände.

I broke the silence, "It is hard to imagine that this was where the party rallies took place."

A child was throwing breadcrumbs to a group of ducks.

"It must be over there ..." I pointed to the rubble of the Luitpoldhalle ... "where Hitler spoke on the 12th September, when he promised the destruction of Czechoslovakia. Today it all looks like an overgrown ruin in a Piranesi engraving."

"But this is not ancient history." The priest interrupted me sharply. "The suffering goes on. Worse than the war is what was done to our people after the war in the name of justice.

The criminals of Dresden and Hiroshima have taken on the role of judge and executioner, with the Czechs as their hangman."

The elderly priest's muscles seem to tighten. A nerve at the corner of his mouth twitched as he went on. "I have spoken to many hundreds of refugees from the Sudetenland, from Silesia, East Prussia. I have seen their pale, empty expressions. I have spoken to the mother of a ten-year-old girl infected with gonorrhoea, raped by the heirs of John Huss."

He told me of the hundreds of letters he had received from Sudeten Germans driven from Czechoslovakia.

"This was a terrible war crime and it must be accounted for."

I felt the landscape close in around me and time fall away. The priest continued, his voice gathering pace.

"Instead, all the Czechs ever talk about is the massacre at Lidice. They have blown that story out of all proportion. It was just one village. This is propaganda. What they did to the Sudeten Germans was a thousand Lidices, and the world won't listen. The Czechs didn't even have a bad war. They were better fed than many Germans. They can't complain."

We took a few steps further. I could feel a slight tension in my throat, not quite sure whether I would be able to speak at all. Above the lapping of the water on the banks of the lake, a hum entered my head, faint but distinct, as if coming from below the surface; it was like the roar of a distant crowd. I forced myself to speak.

"Father Reichenberger, do you remember František Kraus?" My voice was very quiet.

After a short pause he replied, "From the shortwave service of Radiojournal? Of course. Yes. He was a fine man. Is he still alive?"

"Yes. He was in Lidice. He wrote about it."

"How do you mean?" The priest looked uneasy. The air was becoming hard to breathe. "How could he have been?" And after another short silence, "None of the men …"

"He was sent with a group of prisoners from the Terezín Ghetto to bury the men of the village in a mass grave after the SS men from Kladno had shot them. There was an official name for that kind of labour … *Erdarbeiten* … earthworks. It was all quite efficient."

Father Reichenberger listened in silence and I carried on in a flat voice, remembering Kraus's words and speaking as if they were coming from elsewhere.

"When they arrived in an open truck the houses were all still burning with thick black smoke. The bodies of the dead men were lying by a barn wall. Mattresses had been put along the wall to stop the bullets rebounding. The church was on fire."

More of Kraus's account came into my mind

"The opera singer Karel Langendorf was one of the group. As they buried the men he sang from Dvořák's Requiem, almost inaudibly. *Dies irae, dies illa solvet saeclum in favilla …* "

Absently, as if by reflex, Father Reichenberger picked up the words,

"… *teste David et Sibylla …* "

The dimensions of the pit the men were made to dig came into my mind.

"Twelve by nine metres. Four metres deep."

Again we were both silent for a while, the humming continued in my head, and then Father Reichenberger said in a flat tone, not quite a question,

"He was in the Terezín Ghetto, you said. Not the fortress."

I was not quite sure how to interpret his words. The fortress was where the political prisoners had been held, but František Kraus was Jewish and was in the ghetto. Father Reichenberger walked on, restless and nervous. Our steps had chanced to bring us almost to the Zeppelinfeld.

"I am sorry for what happened." The Father had regained his composure. "It is a blessing that Mr Kraus survived."

He was silent for a few seconds, but then went on.

"But why do we only hear about Lidice and the Jews?" He looked at me as if expecting an answer. "And why did Beneš humiliate the Sudeten Germans and drive them into the arms of Hitler? All the time we hear nothing but what was done to the Jews. And no one wants to hear about that ten-year-old girl who was raped by those so-called Czech patriots or the thousands of others like her."

By this time we had reached the very edge of the Zeppelinfeld. My head was pounding. The priest's voice seemed far away.

"And the numbers just don't add up. It is time to take this whole … this episode out of the mists of propaganda. There were three times more Germans murdered than there are Jews on the whole planet."

I looked up towards the shell-scarred ruins. By now the humming was loud and distinct, the rhythmical cheering of a great crowd. The Father was addressing this endless mass. "And what did the supposedly Jew-friendly democracies do before the war to help these poor persecuted people?" There was sarcasm in the Father's voice.

I thought I could hear roars of laughter from the submerged crowd.

"Jew ... friendly ... democracies ... poor ... persecuted ... people," the voices of the crowd echoed in the same rhythm, their mirth by now quite uncontrollable.

The Father's words hung for a moment in the air and then rebounded from the pock-marked limestone slabs of the tribune. The invisible crowd cried back, ecstatic.

Father Reichenberger's last sentence had matched almost perfectly words I had heard from this same tribune on a September evening in 1938.

With a loud, rhythmical splash of its wings a mute swan took off from the lake.

I hardly registered what was happening as the elderly priest shook hands with me politely, smiling gently, as if slightly sorry for me, and we parted. The landscape was silent again, but I felt my head would burst. I sat on the ground beneath a willow tree on the bank of the lake and closed my eyes. It was a long time before I stood up and walked slowly back to my hotel.

*

I know who I WAS when I got up this morning, but I think I must have been changed several times since then.'
'What do you mean by that?' said the Caterpillar sternly.
'Explain yourself!'
'I can't explain myself, I'm afraid, sir' said Alice, 'because I'm not myself, you see.'

*

The next day I was on a train heading towards the Czechoslovak border. I had arranged to act as an interpreter for a group of left-wing clerics from Britain. They were on a pilgrimage to Czechoslovakia to see the country's socialist experiment. I was to join them in Nuremberg having left Britain a few days earlier so that I could have a bit of time in the city. The delegation was led by Hewlett Johnson, the Dean of Canterbury, whom I recognised straight away from a photograph I had seen during the war. It showed him standing outside the Deanery after a Luftwaffe air raid on Canterbury had torn away the front of the building. He had cheerfully carried on living in the ruins for the rest of the war.

Undisciplined long white locks skirted his bald head and despite his solemn priestly garb the impression he gave was anything but serious. He invited me to sit opposite him in the compartment. He talked constantly, animatedly, punctuating the conversation with lively anecdotes. I guessed that he was about the same age as Father Reichenberger.

Our destination was a huge international meeting of Christian clergy of many denominations in the spa town of Luhačovice, on the invitation of the government of the new Czechoslovakia. He handed me a pale blue brochure, with the words *Churches in the Struggle for Peace, 1950*, above a line drawing of a dove.

I told him a little about my time in Prague before the war and was surprised when he told me that he had spent the night of the signing of the Munich Agreement at the Czechoslovak Embassy in London. "I was invited by the Ambassador, Jan Masaryk. A marvellous man. I wish I'd met his father, the president."

I asked how Masaryk had reacted to the news from Munich.

"He was frightfully nervous, constantly pacing the room, smoking one cigarette after another. And he was quite undiplomatic about Chamberlain and Lord Halifax. He said that Halifax was playing the lackey to Hitler and I told him I quite agreed. I felt powerless, ashamed and embarrassed. At the time I vowed that we should never let Czechoslovakia be betrayed again. And that's why I'm here."

As we rumbled through the Bavarian countryside, the Anglican priest spoke enthusiastically about the new order in Czechoslovakia. He talked about the poverty he could remember from the Manchester of his childhood and how it had formed his views on life. "Socialism, with its principle of rewarding each according to his ability, strikes me as being fully in accordance with the basic tenets of Christianity. The criminals of Hiroshima should take a look at the new socialist countries."

The criminals of Hiroshima. Only a few hours earlier Father Reichenberger had used the same term.

Hewlett Johnson continued, "In fact, I think that socialism is the only possible order in this age of machines and technology."

The regular rhythm of the wheels on the tracks seemed to reinforce his message. He went on to talk about the heroes making the steppes and the deserts blossom, and as he spoke he stared intently out of the window, as if the rolling green hills of the Bavarian Forest were being transformed before our eyes.

At the border the train stopped. A Czechoslovak officer in green uniform and high cap came into our compartment, looked at my passport and visa, then disappeared somewhere, taking them with him. After some twenty minutes he came back and accompanied me to a little office in the station, asking me politely to sit down. He sat opposite and opened a file, about an inch thick, that was lying on the desk between us. In broken English he asked me about my role in the delegation, whether I knew any of the delegates personally and what we had talked about on the train. Suddenly he switched to Czech, "You've been here before, haven't you?"

"Yes, before the war," I replied, also in Czech.

As he continued to leaf through the file a faded photograph fell out onto the table. Immediately I recognised myself, Bill Murrow and Gustav Beuer on the square in Liberec on the eve of May Day 1938. I could just make out the fox terrier Pop, before the officer put the photograph back neatly into the file.

"You were in regular contact with the German element."

"I was an interpreter, just as I am now. I also wrote the occasional article for the British papers." I was tempted to add that the German in the picture was a Communist, an anti-Fascist, but somehow I did not think it would help my case.

Where, in heaven's name, had Czechoslovakia's Communist authorities got hold of that picture, taken by Henlein's clumsy would-be spies twelve years and a world war ago? By whatever twist of fate that snapshot came to be here, I think that those lads on the square would have been proud to see their work nicely filed and being put to good use, their legacy being kept alive by like-minded people, albeit in the service of a different set of masters. I wonder if they survived the war.

I was told curtly that I would not be allowed into the country and was asked to remove my luggage from the train. No further explanation was given. The members of the British delegation looked bemused. They passed my two small cases out of the window, a little embarrassed at my plight, but I could see that they were as excited as schoolboys, heading off cheerfully into the unknown without an interpreter. As they steamed out of the station, Hewlett Johnson waved enthusiastically to me from the window.

I had missed the train of history as it headed for a happier future, but to be honest I felt a sense of relief, alone on the platform with nothing but the sound of birdsong from the surrounding forest. My experiences of the last few days had left me dislocated, physically drained, but here in no man's land it was quiet and calm. During the long wait for a return train, my mind kept taking me back to my father when he was dying. I was ten years old and would hold Anna's hand when we visited Papa each day on a huge ward in an anonymous south London hospital. All the patients wore the same grey smocks, stamped with the words *Property of St George's Hospital*. Papa did not recognise us, sometimes he was aggressive, sometimes his words would break down into an incomprehensible mixture of English and German syllables. The doctors told us that his illness had changed his mind. When, after a few days, he drifted into unconsciousness, I felt relief, a little like the relief I felt now. The thread that ties us to what we hold dear is easily broken.

A Voice from the Past

I had never dreamed that one day I would return. It is August 1991 and I am in Czechoslovakia for the first time in over half a century. Since 1950 I have led a quiet life, a bit too quiet, my sister Anna says. I have remained alone and I suppose I am rather set in my ways; too much change bothers me. Out of habit rather than financial need, I continue to translate – contracts and other official documents, although from time to time there is something more interesting, usually from German, occasionally Czech. Often I return to the past, but of late one thing has troubled me more and more. My memories of pre-war Prague have started to break down. Almost imperceptibly, they are being replaced by the ruins of the Zeppelinfeld in 1950 and sometimes I am afraid that before long nothing will remain but its shattered landscapes.

Perhaps that is why I wrote a letter to the shortwave broadcasts of Czechoslovak Radio, and today, to my own surprise, I am here.

Prague has changed remarkably little. The radio building in Fochova – now Vinohradská – Street looks just as it did then, even to the shop selling photographic equipment by the entrance. I have been corresponding with a young Englishman who works for the radio's shortwave service, still going strong after all these years, and now he lets me in. He is slightly awkward and shy in a very English way, but his curiosity appeals to me and I am flattered by the interest he takes in my story. As we chat he reminds me of myself in 1937 when I first arrived here. To the side of the entrance are lists of radio staff who perished in the war, including some I knew.

"We've found the recording you were looking for," he tells me with a grin, before we have even entered the building. "Miraculously, our archive still has lots of recordings from the time before the war." We go into the foyer through the glass doors and I notice that in one place the glass is cracked slightly. The paternoster lift takes us up to the studio, where I am introduced to Daniela, a young studio manager. Her little boy is watching us, swinging his legs to and fro on an office chair in the corner. He sticks his tongue out.

Daniela takes a large reel of quarter-inch tape out of a cardboard sleeve and winds it through the tape machine. The faded typed label on the box states:

E.J. Reichenberger, September 17 1938, catalogue number AF 2286/5.

My walk with Father Reichenberger among the ruins of the Parteigelände in 1950 has been invading my memory, erasing all else. But here, measurable in inches per second, is the short talk that the same Father Reichenberger gave in September 1938, when he was still the Red Chaplain from Liberec and when, as I realise now, he had seen to the depths of the tragedy that was to unfold. At the monitoring station during the war, the memory of his words had helped me every evening to draw back from the hell of the Protectorate.

The tape crackles, clicks, then plays, the voice quite clear, erasing the years between. I am sitting here again with the pre-war Father Reichenberger, listening to his old words, not those that replaced them at our final meeting. Hitler has not yet spread his black wings over Central Europe, breathing his own words into the mouths of those he smothers.

> *I speak as a German who truly loves his people and home and wishes to protect them from destruction. We must not bear the burden of the hatred and curses of the rest of the world. I speak as a human being and a Christian, who sees God's image in every human soul, who believes in worthier ways of settling human and inter-state differences than war and annihilation. I speak as a priest who feels unable to bless weapons which ultimately destroy everyone and everything…*

Simple, unembellished and unsophisticated, the words of a parish priest talking to his congregation.

> *… Everyone must be an apostle of peace, in the home circle, at work, in your daily relationships. Sudeten German men and women: think of your responsibility towards your family before God, your home and our people…*

The words are present in my head as I remember them, and I feel a calm that I have not known for several years. The young Englishman takes me back down to the main entrance, helping me out of the paternoster. Just as we reach the glass doors, two people walk in. I exchange a polite nod with them. "It's the president," the Englishman whispers, gesturing towards the smaller of the two, and for a moment I look round. The cracked glass door closes and a memory returns from a long, long time ago. But I had better stop talking. I feel a tickle in my throat. I'm beginning to lose my voice.

Outside, a tram stops for a moment on the corner of Italská Street. The ten-year-old Danny Silver hops onto the running board, turns and waves. The tram continues up the hill towards Jiřího z Poděbrad, Flora and Olšany.

APPENDIX

The narrator in this story is fictional but the great majority of people he encounters are real and can be found in the many accounts of the period and beyond. A selection of the main characters and their roles is presented here for the more curious reader.

OSWALD BAMBOROUGH: journalist working for the English-language broadcasts of Radiojournal in 1938.

EDVARD BENEŠ: Czechoslovak president, resigned five days after the signing of the Munich Agreement. During WWII Czechoslovak president in London exile. Returned in 1945, but resigned as president after the Communist takeover in 1948 and died three months later.

GUSTAV BEUER: Communist Party deputy in the Czechoslovak National Assembly. A German-speaker from the Sudetenland, after Munich he went into exile in London.

HUBERT BEUVE-MÉRY: correspondent for the French newspaper *Le Temps* in 1938. Resigned from the post after Munich. Later founded *Le Monde*.

KONRAD HENLEIN: the most influential Sudeten German politician of the 1930s. Head of the Sudeten German Party which by 1938 was openly pro-Nazi. Committed suicide in May 1945.

KAREL ČAPEK: Czech playwright, novelist, journalist and democrat. A vocal opponent of all forms of totalitarianism, he died less than three months after Munich.

NEVILLE CHAMBERLAIN: British prime minister (1937–1940). His policy of appeasement led to the signing of the Munich Agreement, which deprived Czechoslovakia of its borderlands.

GEOFFREY COX: New Zealand-born journalist. He was in Prague in 1938 covering events for the *Daily Express*. Later one of the founders of *News at Ten* on British television.

EDOUARD DALADIER: prime minister of France (1938–1940). Co-signatory of the Munich Agreement, which reneged on France's commitment to guarantee Czechoslovakia's borders.

IVAN DÉRER: Slovak Social Democrat and Czechoslovak justice minister at the time of the 1938 crisis. Was involved in the resistance in Prague during the war.

MILOSLAV DISMAN: popular Czech broadcaster before and after the war. Founder of the *Disman Children's Ensemble*.

OTOKAR FISCHER: translator, poet and critic, in 1938 head of drama at the National Theatre in Prague. He died of a heart attack as he heard the news of the Germany's annexation of Austria.

SHIELA GRANT DUFF: British writer and journalist, in Prague in 1938; a strong opponent of appeasement. During the war she worked at the BBC's European Service as the first editor of its Czech section.

JOAN GRIFFIN: anti-appeasement British writer and journalist, working in Prague in 1938 together with her husband …

JONATHAN GRIFFIN: British writer, poet and journalist, working in Prague in 1938. Wartime head of European Intelligence at the BBC.

FRANTIŠEK HALAS: Czech lyric poet, later active in the anti-Nazi resistance. His 1938 collection *Torzo naděje* (*Torso of Hope*), is an appeal to Czechs to stand up to Nazi Germany."

BOŽENA HAVLOVÁ: artist and illustrator. Daughter of Hugo Vavrečka (see below). Her son Václav Havel became Czechoslovakia's first president after the fall of communism in 1989.

MILAN HODŽA: Czechoslovak prime minister (1935–1938), died in wartime exile in the United States.

WENZEL JAKSCH: head of the Sudeten German Social Democrats, spent the war in London exile.

IVAN JELÍNEK: writer, poet and broadcaster. Fled to France in 1939 and then to Britain. After the war worked for many years with the BBC.

MILENA JESENSKÁ: Czech journalist and writer, editor of the prominent political periodical, *Přítomnost*. Died in Ravensbrück in 1944.

HEWLETT JOHNSON: Dean of Canterbury (1931–1963) and a strong supporter of the Soviet Union; known as the "Red Dean".

FRANTA KOCOUREK: prominent pre-war Czech journalist and broadcaster. Arrested in 1941 and murdered in Auschwitz-Birkenau.

FRANTIŠEK KRAUS: writer and broadcaster, pioneer of Czechoslovakia's international broadcasts. Survived Terezín and Auschwitz.

LUDVÍK KREJČÍ: chief of staff of the Czechoslovak armed forces during the Munich Crisis.

ERNST KUNDT: pro-Hitler Sudeten German Party politician. Executed in Prague in 1947.

ALICE MASARYK: founder and head of the Czechoslovak Red Cross after WWI; daughter of the country's first president Tomáš Garrigue Masaryk. In US exile during WWII.

JAN MASARYK: Czechoslovak ambassador to Britain (1925–1938), son of Tomáš Garrigue Masaryk. Foreign minister in the wartime government in exile and after the war. Died under unexplained circumstances two weeks after the 1948 Communist takeover.

SYDNEY "BILL" MORRELL: journalist, writer and strong opponent of appeasement, writing from Prague for the *Daily Express* in 1938. During the war he was an agent for Britain's SOE.

EDWARD R. MURROW: One of the most famous 20th century American broadcasters, best known for his wartime reports from Europe and for challenging Senator McCarthy in 1954. In 1938 he was chief of CBS's European bureau.

VÍTĚZSLAV NEZVAL: Czech writer and poet, co-founder of the Surrealist movement in Czechoslovakia; his 1927 epic poem *Edison* embraces technological innovation but is pessimistic about the future.

EMMANUEL REICHENBERGER: Roman Catholic priest in the Sudetenland, an active opponent of Nazism. He spent the war in the United States and later settled in West Germany.

HUBERT RIPKA: writer, journalist and adviser to President Edvard Beneš. Served in the wartime Czechoslovak government in exile.

W. ROBINSON: journalist. A recording of his voice from 1938 is preserved in the Czech Radio archives, but I have not been able to find out more about him. In the book I have given him the first name Wilfred and have him working in Radiojournal's English broadcasts.

LORD RUNCIMAN: former president of Britain's Board of Trade; led Chamberlain's mission to Czechoslovakia in August 1938 to mediate between the Czechoslovak government and the Sudeten German Party. The mission recommended the transfer of the Sudetenland to Germany.

WILHELM SEBEKOWSKY: a pro-Hitler Sudeten German Party politician and close ally of Konrad Henlein.

VINCENT SHEEAN: American writer and journalist; in Prague in 1938, writing for the *New York Herald Tribune*.

WILLIAM SHIRER: American broadcaster and writer; covered the Austrian Anschluss and the Czechoslovak crisis for CBS. Best known for his reports from Berlin at the beginning of the war.

GORDON SKILLING: Canadian historian; in 1938 he was working on his PhD thesis in Prague and was also employed by the English-language service of Radiojournal. After the war he became a prominent historian of central and eastern Europe.

JAN SLAVÍK: Czech historian. A strong opponent of Nazism, he was extremely wary of historical dogmas. After the war his work was also banned by the Communist regime.

LADISLAV ŠOUREK: Czechoslovak radio pioneer, in 1938 director of Radiojournal.

JAN SYROVÝ: Czechoslovak Army general, WWI hero, nominated prime minister during the Munich Crisis.

OSKAR ULLRICH: spokesman of the pro-Hitler Sudeten German Party in 1938, a close associate of Konrad Henlein.

HUGO VAVREČKA: Czechoslovak politician, appointed propaganda minister during the Munich Crisis in response to Nazi Germany's disinformation campaign. Grandfather of Václav Havel.

EDGAR YOUNG: British left-wing politician and peace activist, visited Czechoslovakia in 1937 and 1938.

ZDENKA WALLÓ: one of the first presenters for Radiojournal's foreign language broadcasts. Murdered in Auschwitz-Birkenau in 1944.

RECENT TITLES PUBLISHED BY JANTAR

Gaudeamus *by* RICHARD

Translated by David Short

"All crimes, great and small, finally lead to murder."

Based on real events.
The unloved wife of a doctor practising in Slovakia comes across his medical notes after his death. One 'unofficial patient' has severe problems coming to terms with the disappearance and murder of his childhood sweetheart. Set in Slovakia from the mid-1970s onwards, historical fact, murder, loss and mourning combine delicately in a tale of love, loss, redemption and joy.

-- ISBN: 978-0-9933773-4-1

Three Plastic Rooms *by* PETRA HŮLOVÁ

Translated by Alex Zucker, with an introduction by Peter Zusi

A foul-mouthed Prague prostitute muses on her profession, aging and the nature of materialism. She explains her world view in the scripts and commentaries of her own reality TV series combining the mundane with fetishism, violence, wit and an unvarnished mixture of vulgar and poetic language.

-- ISBN: 978-0-9933773-9-6

Children of Our Age *by* A. M. BAKALAR

Karol and his wife are the rising stars of the Polish community in London but Karol is a ruthless entrepreneur whose fortune is built on the backs of his fellow countrymen. The Kulesza brothers, mentally unstable Igor and his violent brother Damian, dream about returning to Poland one day. A loving couple, Mateusz and Angelika, believe against all odds that good things will happen to people like them. Gradually, all of these lives become dramatically entwined, and each of them will have to decide how far they are willing to go in pursuit of their dreams.

Insightful and unforgiving, *Children of Our Age* is a deeply human and timely story of Polish immigrants. Sweeping between their past in Poland and their present in Britain, this electrifying novel explores the ways unlikely encounters transform lives, the limits of loyalty, and love.

--ISBN: 978-0-9933773-3-4

For further news on new books and events, please visit
www.JantarPublishing.com